MARGARET MO

◆

THE LOMBARDI EMERALDS

Complete and Unabridged

LINFORD
Leicester

First published in Great Britain in 2020

First Linford Edition
published 2021

A catalogue record for this book is available
from the British Library.

ISBN 978–1–4448–4708–6

Published by
Ulverscroft Limited
Anstey, Leicestershire

Set by Words & Graphics Ltd.
Anstey, Leicestershire
Printed and bound in Great Britain by
TJ Books Ltd., Padstow, Cornwall

This book is printed on acid-free paper

THE LOMBARDI EMERALDS

Who is Auguste Lombardi, and why has May's mother been invited to his eightieth birthday party? As her mother is halfway to Australia, and May is resting between acting roles, she attends in her place. To celebrate the occasion, she wears the earrings her mother gave her for her birthday – only to discover that they are not costume jewellery, but genuine emeralds, and part of the famous missing Lombardi collection . . .

No Admittance

'Sorry, darling, you know how it is — showbiz.'

Archie Fisher's words echoed in May Maxwell's ears as she peered through the wrought iron railings bordering the manicured gardens of the Villa Lombardi. There was no-one around. She wasn't even sure she was in the right place.

The late morning sun beat down on her back and she was glad she had chosen to wear her biggest straw hat. Her flimsy sundress afforded little protection against the fierce Mediterranean sun and she could feel her skin prickling in protest.

If it hadn't been for Archie Fisher she wouldn't be here now, but Archie Fisher was yesterday. She wouldn't waste any more time thinking about him.

May straightened her shoulders and turned her attention back to the villa. Its blue shutters were closed against the sun's intense heat and the emblazoned flag on the roof curled lazily around its pole as if it couldn't summon up the energy to flap and display the distinctive family crest — a red dragon breathing flames at a rock against a background of deep blue sea.

As May stepped back she heard the throaty roar of an approaching car racing up the hill.

She scooted towards a convenient classical Roman statue that appeared to be guarding the premises and, using the senator's toga as cover, she peered out from her hiding place and watched the gates creak open to admit the driver after she identified herself to the security monitor.

The smell of exhaust fumes diminished as the sports car headed towards the Baroque villa. May watched the driver park by the ornamental fountain then stride up the front steps of the house before disappearing through the impressive main door that had been opened pending her arrival.

May hesitated. Would she get the same reception? Clutching her invitation, she strode confidently towards the gates. Startled to see her image leap into life on the monitor attached to the top of the railings, she paused.

'May Maxwell,' she announced in a positive voice. Her identity statement was met with a crackle and a request to repeat her name. After an unnerving wait she was informed her name was not on the list and her image disappeared from the screen. Fuming, she glared at the monitor and pressed the button again. There was no response.

She looked down at the scrawled note on the invitation she was clutching.

'One last gig,' she read.

The invitation was embossed, old-fashioned, gold edged and printed in flourishing script on expensive stationery, the sort that didn't bend after being crammed into a handbag for several hours.

May had never heard of Auguste Lombardi and she hadn't been sure what to do with the invitation. In normal circumstances she would probably have ignored it but after losing out on a plum acting role because the producer wanted his niece to have the part for which she had been cast she knew she absolutely had to get away from Limester and the invitation to attend Auguste Lombardi's eightieth birthday celebrations had arrived at exactly the right time, even if it wasn't addressed to her.

After a brief battle with her conscience she had decided not to tell her mother about the invitation. Tish was on her way to Australia and May reasoned she couldn't possibly come back in time for the party.

A voice made May jump.

'What do you want?' The uniformed guard sounded unfriendly.

'My name is May Maxwell,' she began again.

'No visitors,' the guard insisted in a menacing voice before turning on his heel and retreating to the discreetly positioned security box.

4

'Hey, come back,' she called after him.

Fuming as he continued to ignore her, May swung round and collided with a man standing behind her.

'Prego.' He stepped aside. 'Vincenzo Piace.' He bowed.

'Are you a member of the family?' May demanded.

'Why do you wish to know?'

'Can you get me admitted to the villa? I have an invitation.'

'Not if your name is not on the list,' he repeated the guard's words. 'Is it on the list?'

'No,' May was forced to admit.

'Then I cannot help you. Signor Lombardi takes his security very seriously.'

'I suppose it's too late to introduce myself as Tish Delacourt?' May asked.

'I thought you told the guard your name was May Maxwell.'

'It is.' She hesitated. 'It's a long story.'

'Which unfortunately I do not have time to hear right now.'

As they were speaking, a taxi drew up. A sulky-faced, slender girl emerged and, running towards Vincenzo, flung her arms around him.

'I am not too late for Auguste's brunch, am I?' She released him from her embrace, the sulky look replaced with a calculating smile.

'My car wouldn't start so I had to call a taxi,' she gestured towards the driver, 'which was late, then he chose to come the long way round. I thought I would never get here. The traffic in the market was unbearable.'

'You're here now, Rebecca, so no worries. Why don't you go on in and join the others?'

Rebecca linked her arm through Vincenzo's.

'Let's get the show on the road.' She smiled up at him. 'But I was forgetting — my gift.' She ran back to the taxi and retrieved a small shiny packet from the back seat. 'It's a handkerchief, pure silk, lemon, Nonno's favourite colour. I picked it up on our way through the market.'

May's knowledge of Italian was

sketchy but she seemed to recall nonno translated as grandfather.

So this was Auguste's granddaughter. Her apricot wrap-over dress clung to her tanned limbs in all the right places and by May's reckoning cost a lot more than her own dress that had seen at least three summers and would probably see a few more before she parted with it.

In the background she heard the taxi driver speak rapidly into his radio before starting up his engine.

'Wait.' May leaped forward and yanked open the rear passenger door. 'Pensione Betta,' she said, leaping into the back seat. 'Can you take me there?'

With a reluctant shrug the driver acknowledged her presence and after a violent lurch they headed off down the hill in the direction of Bella Acqua.

'Who was that?' Rebecca asked as the taxi drove away.

'May Maxwell,' Vin replied with a thoughtful look, 'and I have a feeling we haven't heard the last of her.'

As May settled back in the rear seat

of the musty smelling taxi she realised to her dismay she had dropped her invitation.

'Can we turn back?' May gestured at the driver who refused to meet her eye in the rear view mirror. She tapped him on the shoulder, receiving an unhelpful grunt in reply as he put his foot down harder on the accelerator.

Swallowing the lump of disappointment rising in her throat, May leaned back against the sun-scorched seat and closed her eyes, accepting the inevitable. It was time to let fate take over her future. She had totally run out of options.

Secrets and Rumours

'They no let you in?' Salvadore was all commiseration. 'I ask Betta to prepare some special doughnuts. You need sugar for the shock.' He bustled off in search of his wife.

May sank into one of the cushioned cane chairs on the terrace of the *pensione* and inhaled the honeysuckle fragrance of the trailing bougainvillea as she tried to come to terms with the happenings of the morning.

She needed to think. If she was careful she had enough money to last for a month or so but in the meantime how was she going to gain access to Sr Lombardi?

She tried to recall the exact wordin on her mother's invitation. Someor called Florence Amaria had invited Tis Delacourt to Auguste Lombardi's eigh ieth birthday party celebrations and ha added a handwritten plea suggesting o:

last gig.

Who was Florence Amaria, May mused and Tish Delacourt — what was all that about? Her mother's name was Tish Maxwell. If May hadn't dropped her invitation she would have had another go at gaining access to the villa. It was the sole link she had to her past and with her mother on the high seas and not able to interfere she knew she wouldn't get another chance like this.

It was going to be a challenge as it was. Tish would soon start getting suspicious and demand to know why May hadn't Skyped her and there was no way she could disguise her room at the Pensione Betta to look like her bedsit in Limester. May was going to have to work fast if she wanted results.

Her conscience told her she should have ignored the invitation but Tish had a secret and May was determined to find out about it. Her father was the one subject Tish absolutely refused to discuss with her, even though May kept insisting she had a right to know. She had tried asking her grandparents but they were none the wiser.

'I don't like to see Tish upset.' Coco had delivered a rare reprimand when one of her and May's exchanges had grown more heated than usual. 'And your raised voices are disturbing your grandfather.'

After their last clash, May had been reluctant to raise the matter again.

She leaned back against her cushion and closed her eyes. She could hear the market stallholders calling to each other as they closed up for the day. The smell of freshly percolated coffee alerted her to Betta's presence as the older woman appeared on the terrace, carrying a loaded tray.

'Salvadore tell me what happened.' Her face was red from talking and holding the tray at the same time. She raised her shoulders in a gesture of despair. 'It does not surprise me.'

'Let me.' May leaped to her feet and helped her unload doughnuts and coffee.

'You know the Lombardis?' she asked

when they had both settled down.

'We do not mix socially. They are society people.'

'Can you tell me anything about them?'

A pensive look crossed Betta's face.

'There is no-one left but Auguste now,' she said, a trace of compassion in her voice.

May raised a questioning eyebrow. She sensed Betta liked to gossip and that it wouldn't take much persuasion to get her to talk about the Lombardi family.

'I do not discuss people behind their back,' Betta insisted.

'I understand.' May went along with her unconvincing response and waited for Betta to continue.

'I don't know where to start.' The older woman wriggled into a more comfortable position in her seat opposite May. 'Auguste Lombardi is a very elegant man — sophisticated, too.'

'Have you met him?'

'Several times in the past but recently he has been unwell and now rarely ventures far from the villa.'

'I am sorry to hear that.'

'Don't be. The family is tainted with scandal. You are better off without them.'

May's heart sank.

'But I do not like to gossip,' Betta repeated.

'Then you cannot tell me anything?' To cover her disappointment, May bit into a pastry.

Betta appeared to battle with her conscience before rising to the bait.

'The family were big in racing cars. That's where the money came from.'

'Racing cars?' May repeated.

'Your family are big in racing cars, too?'

May shook her head. Tish had no absolutely no interest in anything mechanical and her grandfather had been a carpenter.

'I'm afraid not.'

Betta nodded as if she had expected as much. May wasn't sure what answer she would give if Betta persisted with her line of questioning. She still had no idea why her mother had been invited to Sr Lombardi's party or why she would never talk about her time in Italy.

'You said Sr Lombardi was alone now.' May risked another question.

'Auguste had one son, Hector. Hector was a playboy like his father had been before his marriage.'

'I see.'

'Auguste liked to mix with a glamorous set then he met the beautiful Giovanna Lago — La Principessa.'

'She was royalty?' May gulped.

'She was not a princess, but it was what Auguste called her. She was the love of his life. Her family crest is displayed on the flag at the villa. You have seen it?'

'The fire-breathing dragon?'

Betta nodded.

'Giovanna was aristocracy, but she was also delicate. The summer heat was too much for her constitution. She was rarely seen in the village, especially after Hector was born.'

'What happened?'

'She faded away and Auguste was

never the same again. He was overcome with grief and for a while he shut himself away too. Young Hector ran wild. There was no-one to stop him. Without his mother's love and a father's protection he did as he pleased.'

'What a sad story,' May said.

'More coffee?' Betta asked.

May shook her head but helped herself to another doughnut, uncertain where her next meal would be coming from.

'You are a friend of Sr Lombardi?' Betta asked the question May had been dreading.

'The birthday invitation was sent to a relation.' May decided to stick to as much of the truth as she dared. 'I am here as family representative but as my name was not on the official list of guests . . . ' She paused.

'They don't let you in.' May nodded as if it was what she would have expected. 'It is a pity. The gardens are beautiful this time of year and I believe there will be a week of celebrations.'

'Do you know Florence Amaria?' May

asked.

'Everyone knows everyone in Bella Acqua.' Betta didn't meet May's eyes. 'It is a small community,' she added.

'What is Ms Amaria's connection to Sr Lombardi?'

'It is personal,' Betta said, the expression on her face indicating further questions on the subject weren't welcome. 'Now I must get on.'

'What happened to Hector?' May persisted.

'It is not something I like to talk about.'

May held out her coffee cup.

'I think I will have a refill after all,' she said.

'You have a healthy appetite.' Betta eyed up the empty plate of doughnuts. 'My granddaughter — she eat nothing except salad leaves.'

'I should eat a few more salad leaves,' May replied.

'That is not true.' Betta bridled, looking down at her own ample figure. 'Food is there for us to enjoy. You like my doughnuts because they give you pleasure.'

16

'Hector Lombardi?' May coaxed, hoping now she was back in Betta's good books she would get an answer.

Betta paused.

'The mountain roads here can be dangerous,' she said. 'It happened at the height of the summer season. It was a warm day and Hector was out in his car. No-one knows where he was going. The story was he took one bend too fast and lost control. There was big trouble but the affair was hushed up. Of course there were rumours. Hector was said to be racing another car and that was the reason for the crash.'

'But I thought Sr Lombardi had a granddaughter called Rebecca,' May said, remembering the slender girl whose taxi she had taken back to the village.

'Betta,' Salvadore called through from the kitchen, 'phone.'

Betta scrambled to her feet, as if fearing she had said too much, and left May alone on the terrace with her thoughts.

What had her mother been doing in Italy? May been born in Milan but Tish would never explain why.

Her grandparents were from the West Country. They liked to live quietly and never travelled far from home. It didn't make sense. The questions went round and round May's head until a buzz from her mobile broke into her thoughts. A text from Coco brought a smile to her face.

Until a few years ago her grandmother would have nothing to do with technology but now like all converts she embraced social media with enthusiasm. Her text was full of smiley emoticons.

'U have to try the life, dancing every nite, painting classes, Spanish lessons and lots of suitable escorts.'

Her message signed off with rows of kisses and love hearts.

'You have a visitor,' Betta interrupted as May tapped out her reply.

She looked up in startled surprise as she saw Vincenzo Piace standing in the doorway.

Unwelcome Proposal

'You dropped this.' Vin produced her crumpled invitation out of his pocket.

May put out a hand to snatch it out of his grasp but he held it out of her reach.

'It's mine. Can I have it back?'

'If your name is Tish Delacourt.'

'You know it isn't.'

'Then you have your answer.'

May stifled the urge to say what she thought of his behaviour. Vin might provide a lead to her past and it wouldn't do to make an enemy of him. He was frowning at her as if he couldn't quite make out what she was doing here and right now May felt exactly the same.

'Thank you for returning my invitation,' she said, 'I would like to keep it as a souvenir.'

'Not so fast.' He continued to hang on to it.

'I beg your pardon?'

'You tried to gain access to the Villa

Lombardi.'

'You know I did.'

'Under a false identity.' Vin spoke slowly and carefully and when May didn't respond he persisted. 'Didn't you?'

May tossed her head, refusing to be intimidated by his interrogation.

'What if I did?'

'Why are you so keen to attend a party to which you have not been invited?'

'I don't have to answer your questions.'

The intense scrutiny of his dark brown eyes was making it difficult to act casual.

'Yes you do,' Vin insisted, barring May's path as she tried to leave the terrace.

'Excuse me.'

'A few more moments of your time if you would be so kind.' Vin did not budge, the tone of his voice suggesting it wasn't a request but an order.

'Since we're playing the truth game, here's a question for you,' May fired back at him. 'What is your connection to Sr Lombardi?'

'Sr Piace is Sr Lombardi's right-hand

man. Can I offer you some refreshment?' Betta asked her visitor as she finished her telephone call.

Vin flashed her a smile that completely changed his facial expression. May wished he would smile at her in the same way. It would make her predicament a lot easier to bear.

'Thank you, Betta. No-one in Bella Acqua makes better orange juice than you.'

'Right away,' Betta responded with what amounted to a girlish smile.

'So you're Sr Lombardi's right-hand man,' May said after Betta had gone in search of fresh orange juice.

'That is correct, and I want to know what you were doing snooping around the villa.'

'I was not snooping.'

'I was watching you. You peered through the gates, hid behind a statue when you heard a car arriving, then you approached the gates again but the guard on duty refused you entry.'

The thought of Vin Piace spying on

her was unsettling and May hadn't realised she had been quite so obvious.

'You have been busy,' she said.

'Please,' Vin indicated the seat she had recently vacated, 'sit down.'

Betta's return created a welcome interruption and May watched Vin relieve her of the jug of orange juice and two glasses. He was, she guessed, about thirty years old.

His muscular build suggested he didn't spend his days seated behind a desk. His fingernails, although short, bore evidence of a dark substance, possibly motor oil. She remembered Betta had mentioned racing cars were the source of the Lombardi fortune.

'I wish to know what you were doing at the villa,' Vin demanded, after Betta had left the terrace. 'I am asking because attempts have been made in the past to kidnap Sr Lombardi.'

May's mouth fell open in surprise. Accusations of that nature were the last thing she had been expecting.

'I can assure you I had no intention of

abducting Sr Lombardi, nor was I casing the joint,' she insisted.

'How did you manage to get hold of an invitation addressed to Tish Delacourt?'

'Do you know Tish Delacourt?' May countered, playing for time.

'I don't but if you are as innocent as you say you are then answering my question shouldn't be a problem.'

'*Mi scusi.*' Betta was back, looking a little red in the face. 'I do not listen at the door.'

May cast Vin a disbelieving look and saw to her surprise her expression mirrored in his amused eyes.

'Go on, Betta,' he invited with a wry smile.

'You remember the telephone call Salvadore took before Sr Piace arrive?' She looked at May. 'It was to confirm a block booking. From tomorrow your room will no longer be available at the pensione.'

'Is there nowhere else for me to stay?'

May was starting to feel desperate. Fate appeared to be conspiring against her.

'I was thinking perhaps Sr Piace could offer you a room at the villa as Sr Lombardi's guest? That way he could keep an eye on you.'

'Good idea.' Vin pounced on Betta's suggestion.

'Hang on a moment,' May could feel panic rising in her chest, 'don't I have a say in the matter?'

'You do,' Vin conceded, 'and I would be pleased to hear it.'

May was annoyed to see Vin found her discomfort a source of amusement.

'I don't accept your offer.'

'Why not? You're desperate to meet Sr Lombardi, aren't you?'

'You have accused me of assuming a false identity in order to get to see Sr Lombardi — possibly with a view to kidnapping him.'

'That is true.'

'Do I look like a bandit?' May was growing exasperated. If the situation weren't so serious she too would find it funny.

'I don't believe I actually accused you

of trying to kidnap Sr Lombardi.'

'All the same, why are you offering me a room at the villa?'

'Isn't there a saying about keeping your friends close and your enemies closer still?'

Vin taunted.

'I am not your enemy.'

'In which case,' Betta joked, 'you can be friends.'

May's colour deepened. There was something seriously disquieting about Vin Piace, disquieting enough for her not to want to be his friend or to be in his debt.

'What if I turn down your offer?'

'I will alert the authorities to your presence in Bella Acqua and suggest they investigate your background. Sr Lombardi is an influential man. They will not ignore him.'

'I haven't done anything wrong.'

'Then you can explain to the authorities.'

The expression on Vin's face reminded May of a cat taunting a mouse.

'If I accept your proposal . . . ' May mused, thinking on her feet.

'Yes?' Vin encouraged.

'You're not planning on doing anything illegal?'

'Such as?'

'Locking me up.'

'You have my solemn promise you will be free to come and go as you wish.'

'And do I also have your promise you will not try to contact Tish Delacourt?'

There was a disturbance in the corner of the room.

'Salvadore needs me.' Betta looked red in the face as if not wanting to play any more part in the proceedings. 'We have much to do to prepare for our new guests.' She hurried out of the room.

Ignoring Betta's outburst, Vin replied to May's question.

'No doubt you have your reasons for making such a request.'

'I do.'

'And you won't tell me why?'

'No.'

'Do you have any other demands?'

'If you don't accept my conditions I am prepared to take my chances with the local authorities.' May crossed her arms in a gesture of triumph. 'So it's your call.'

Vin swirled his orange juice around the bottom of his glass.

'I agree to your terms,' he said.

'Do you?' May closed her eyes in relief. She hoped she had done the right thing because it was too late to back out now.

'Be ready by ten o'clock tomorrow morning.'

'How do you know I won't disappear during the night?' May couldn't help asking.

'I don't,' he admitted, 'but from my knowledge of human nature when someone wants something badly they are prepared to enter the lion's den, and you very badly want to see Sr Lombardi, don't you?'

May blinked and lowered her eyes. Vin picked up his car keys.

'One last request,' he said.

May raised her eyes.

'I need your word that you do not

intend to harm Sr Lombardi in any way, either physically or emotionally.'

May hesitated. The question was a tough one. How was she going to find out about her mother's connection to the Villa Lombardi without upsetting someone?

'You have my word.'

She hoped her reply would not come back to haunt her.

'I will see you tomorrow.'

May looked down at her mother's invitation. Vin had left it on the coffee table. The words 'one last gig' danced in front of her eyes as she heard Vin drive away.

A Different World

May basked in the sunshine while she sat on the step outside the Pensione Betta the next morning, watching the early sun paint patterns on the cobblestone street. The clock in the church tower chimed 10 as Vin drove up.

'Good.' He nodded approval as he swung her suitcase into the boot of his car and held open the passenger door, 'Sr Lombardi does not like to be kept waiting.'

'He wants to see me now?' May's heartbeat trebled.

In all the confusion she hadn't prepared a back up story and she had no idea what she was going to say to him. She'd had very little sleep the night before, her restless conscience going into overdrive as she battled with the enormity of what she had done behind her mother's back and how Tish would react when she eventually found out.

'It's as well to be prepared,' Vin replied to May's question. 'I have told him about you and he is looking forward to meeting you. You are happy with the top down?' Vin asked as he settled down behind the steering wheel and started the engine.

He was wearing smart casual — short-sleeved shirt and crisp chinos. His forearms were suntanned as if he spent long hours working outside and May wondered exactly what his duties entailed.

'Thank you.' She was feeling more like her usual self after a breakfast of croissants and ripe peaches on Betta's terrace. 'It's a lovely day,' she added in an attempt to lighten any atmosphere lingering over from yesterday's encounter.

Vin flashed a smile in her direction.

'You don't mind if I drive fast? I won't exceed the limit, but there is very little traffic out this early in the morning and I like to open up the throttle to get the best out of the engine.'

Vin's safe but swift driving erased May's memory of her journey with the surly driver in his unpleasant-smelling taxi. The touch of the warm sun on her face and tang of rosemary and mint in the morning air revitalised her jaded senses and for the first time since she had arrived in Bella Acqua she felt faintly optimistic about the future.

The guards had opened the gates by the time Vin reached the villa and May couldn't help sweeping a triumphant glance at the official who had barred her entry. Today they drove through without a hitch. Vin drove round the back of the villa to a small studio surrounded by a sea of flowers — oleander, alpine asters and brilliant blue cornflowers.

'You'll be staying here,' he explained as he hefted May's suitcase out of the boot. 'Auguste's wife Giovanna used the studio as her personal refuge when she needed time alone. Gardening was one of her passions.'

'It reminds me of my grandmother's garden.' May hoped Coco's next-door neighbour was remembering to water the rockery in the family's absence.

'Glad you like it.' Vin flashed another

of his brief smiles.

A uniformed member of staff appeared and collected May's suitcase.

'We've a whole week of festivities arranged,' he explained. 'Someone will call for you before the start of the evening celebrations. You'll find everything you need inside and if you don't, just ask. *Ciao*.'

Vin reversed his car and drove away as swiftly as he had arrived before May could ask any further questions.

She ventured into the cool solitude of the studio, marvelling at the luxury of the facilities. A claw-foot tub dominated the bathroom, which boasted fluffy towels, toiletries and an extensive vanity area. In the bedroom, an ethnic throw covered a huge bed and on the floor a display of woollen weave scatter rugs added a splash of colour to the rustic wooden furnishings.

Headed up with the familiar red dragon crest, a printed programme of events itemising the various activities arranged to celebrate Sr Lombardi's eightieth birthday had been placed on the throw. Tonight's party was to be a buffet supper on the terrace.

May scanned the list of activities. It included classical concerts, piano concertos and a violin sonata. May tapped the programme thoughtfully against the back of her thumb. This sort of thing was not Tish's scene at all. She didn't think she had ever seen her mother in what she would term grown-up clothes. Tish favoured a relaxed style of fashion and her personal life reflected her tastes.

She wasn't into designer bath oils and expensive furnishings or classical concerts and she certainly did not mix with European aristocracy.

May took off her shoes and stretched out on the bed, closing her eyes. A gentle tapping on the door roused her. She realised to her consternation she had been asleep for several hours.

A housemaid delivered a light afternoon snack on a tray. Seeing May's suitcase was still on the floor she proceeded to unpack her meagre wardrobe.

May flushed as the maid hung her peasant style skirts and summer tops in the cavernous wardrobe.

Still smiling, the maid dealt with her other items of luggage before indicating a second wardrobe. Opening the door she produced a cream shift dress, plain apart from a decorative bow on the hip and a pair of matching high heeled sandals, a style of footwear May never wore.

Pointing to the invitation, the maid indicated May was to wear this dress for the evening party.

May scrambled off the bed and inspected the dress hanging on the wardrobe door. Things were getting more confusing by the minute. Why had Sr Lombardi's staff thought it necessary to provide her with a dress to wear for his birthday celebrations?

As she asked herself the question her lips twisted into a wry smile. She had to acknowledge the dresses she had brought with her would be hopelessly inappropriate for such an occasion, and if she wanted to carry on with her investigations she was going to have to fall in with Sr Lombardi's plans.

Showering and blow-drying her hair, she decided to twist it up in a chignon. When she was resting May liked to keep make-up to a minimum. However, tonight had to be the exception to the rule. She smudged smoky grey eye shadow on to her eyelids and keeping her hand steady applied mascara to her lashes. The woman who looked back at her in the mirror took her breath away. A European sophisticate had replaced jobbing actress May Maxwell.

Her aquamarine eyes flashed a message she did not understand. Had the dress done this to her? Could clothes and make-up change a personality? In a spirit of defiance she extracted a pair of earrings from her bag. Her mother had given them to her on her twenty-third birthday two years earlier.

'I named you after the month you were born, my darling,' she had said, 'and emeralds are your birthstone. I am sorry they are costume but I couldn't afford the real thing.'

May fingered the delicate anemone-shaped faux diamond and emerald earrings before fixing them in her ears. With her confidence bolstered she took a deep breath and answered a discreet tap on the door. A uniformed maid was waiting dutifully outside.

Following her through the camellia garden, May reminded herself it was important not to get carried away by dresses and designer accessories. Tonight was her big chance to find out exactly what was the connection between her mother and the Villa Lombardi. That was all that mattered.

* * *

Pineapple lights were strung in the trees, their bright colours reflected in the inky darkness of the lake. The private landing stage was lit with flaming torches positioned at convenient intervals to guide the guests along the deck and up to the house. Gentle water slapped the sides

36

of the jostling boats as yet more arrivals disembarked.

'It's like something out of a fairy tale,' May said to the maid as they circuited the house.

The maid left her in the care of another attendant who handed her a wrap.

May had not realised she was shivering, whether it was from the cool night air or a premonition of what was to come she wasn't sure, but she accepted the peacock blue silk shawl with a smile and draped it around her shoulders. Clutching the fringed edge helped to steady her nervous hands.

She saw a small group of guests gathered around an elderly gentleman. He was dressed in a white-jacketed dinner suit. It emphasised his tan and with his swept back grey hair May could see in his youth he had been outstandingly handsome. He exuded an air of power and authority and May was convinced this was Sr Lombardi. As he glanced up at her she walked towards him. She could feel his eyes fixed on her and drawing on her drama school training May placed one leg carefully in front of the other and looking straight ahead willed her body not to tremble. A figure materialised out of the shadows. Vin Piace was dressed in a dinner suit but unlike Auguste Lombardi his tie was slightly crooked. May longed to tell him but before she could speak he took hold of her elbow.

'You're ready?' His eyes swept over her appearance.

Feeling like a puppet being pulled in directions she wasn't sure she wanted to go, May was grateful for the strength of Vin's arm against hers.

'Yes,' she said summoning up a light smile.

'Good,' he acknowledged. 'Let me introduce you to Sr Lombardi.'

Hostile Reception

As introductions went, it was a disappointment. After a brief glance in her
direction and an acknowledgement of
her presence, Sr Lombardi waved her
away. Deflated, May allowed Vin to lead
her to the buffet table. He handed over
a flute of champagne and chinked his
glass against hers.

'That went well,' he said in a quiet
voice. 'Sr Lombardi does not usually
take to outsiders,' he explained.

'Why not? May frowned.

'For various reasons.' Vin paused.
'You're not a journalist, are you? I should
have asked earlier.'

'I'm an actress.'

'And are you acting a part now?' Vin
asked.

'I suppose I am,' May replied. 'I mean
I don't belong here.'

'Where do you belong?'

'Limester. Have you been to England?'

'Once many years ago on a school trip to London.'

'Limester is a small West Country community not far from the sea.'

'I like the sound of it.' Vin's reply surprised May. 'I grew up in an Italian village where you were liked for who you were, not for what you had in life.'

May sensed that, like her, Vin wasn't totally at ease in such a glamorous setting. He showed no inclination of wanting to leave May's side to mingle with the other guests for which she was grateful.

From the snatches of conversation she had overheard, the talk seemed to concern mutual friends, private parties, yachts, villas and a life very far removed from her own.

'The young lady seated next to Sr Lombardi,' May felt emboldened to ask, 'who is she? I saw her yesterday getting out of a taxi.'

'Her name is Rebecca Amaria.'

May felt a quickening of her pulse.

'Is she related to Florence Amaria?'

'She is her daughter.'

'And it was Florence who arranged this party?'

'She did,' Vin replied, not volunteering further details.

May decided to change the subject.

'Can you tell me what you do for a living?'

'You know what I do for a living. I am Sr Lombardi's right-hand man.'

'You've got oil under your fingernails and I'm willing to say there aren't many people here who work with their hands.'

Vin glanced down at the stains, a wry smile twisting his lips.

'No matter how hard I try it never seems to come off. I'm sorry if oil offends you.'

'It doesn't,' May said. 'My grandfather was a carpenter and he always smelt of varnish. Coco was always complaining she could never get her towels clean.'

'Coco?'

'My grandmother. Her real name is Caroline but Coco was a childhood nickname that stuck.'

41

'Did you have a happy childhood?' Vin looked as though he was interested in May's answer and not merely making polite conversation.

'Yes, very. With my mother away a lot my grandparents gave me free rein to more or less do as I pleased.'

'A philosophy you seem to have adopted in adult life,' Vin remarked.

Before May could respond, a woman tapped him on the shoulder.

'Vin, darling, you absolutely have to come and meet my latest. He has bought a new car and he's dying to tell you all about it.' She moved in closer to him but didn't extend the invitation to May.

'Don't mind me.' May gestured with her champagne glass. 'I'll find someone to talk to, I'm sure.'

Wandering over to the balustrade, May watched the colourful reflections from the fairy lights swirl patterns in the water, its surface disturbed by the arrival of yet more limousines delivering guests.

May rubbed her foot against the back of her leg to ease the pressure in her toes. Her glittery sandals were very glamorous but hard work. She would have liked to sit down but all the chairs were occupied and she didn't have the confidence to gatecrash any of the groups chatting about the latest fashions or their business deals.

A light breeze disturbed her chignon and she put a hand up to her hair to tweak it back into place, her palm brushing against her ear lobe. She tweaked the loose clasp of her earring back into place as her thoughts reverted to Sr Lombardi. She wondered how he had been talked into allowing her to stay over in his beloved wife's studio. Given his aversion to strangers it seemed odd he should allow someone he did not know to use it.

With these thoughts whirling around her head she didn't immediately notice someone standing beside her until a shadow fell across the water. It was Rebecca. Her upper lip curled unpleasantly as she regarded May with an unfriendly gleam in her cat like eyes.

'What are you doing here?' she

demanded.

'I have an invitation,' May replied in as pleasant a voice as she could manage.

'I do not know you.'

'And I do not know you,' May countered.

'I heard you ask Vin about me.'

'I asked because I saw you arriving yesterday in a taxi.'

'Vin told me you tried to sneak into Nonno's brunch.'

'I had an invitation.'

'You stole an invitation.' Rebecca spat the words at May.

May feared the situation could get awkward. One or two of the guests glanced in their direction.

'I'm going to get you evicted.'

'You are not being very polite to a guest,' a voice interrupted the exchange.

An elegant woman extended a hand towards May.

'Sofia Napoli. I am named after the beautiful city.' She laughed.

'May Maxwell,' May replied.

'Maxwell?' Sofia repeated the name

slowly. 'I don't think I know the name.'

'No-one's heard of her,' Rebecca intervened.

'Because we do not know someone there is no reason to be rude to them,' Sofia reprimanded her.

She turned her attention back to May. 'Is this your first time in Italy?' she asked.

'I was born here.'

Sofia raised an eyebrow.

'May I ask where?'

'Milan.'

'Please don't think I am now the one who is being rude,' Sofia's smile curved her lips, 'but may I ask you another question?'

'I don't have to answer it if I don't want to.'

'I see we speak the same language,' Sofia responded with a friendly smile. 'From where did you acquire your earrings?' she asked.

'They were a birthday present from my mother.'

'Were they indeed?' Sofia looked

thoughtful. 'They are exquisite. I don't think I have seen anything so beautiful in a long time. I suggest you take great care of them.'

With a slight acknowledgement of her head towards Rebecca she drifted away.

'You needn't think Vin is available.' Rebecca renewed her verbal attack on May. 'I am going to marry him.'

May did her best to conceal her surprise. The age gap had to be a significant one and from what she knew of Vin she was sure he wouldn't suffer fools gladly. Rebecca, if not exactly behaving foolishly, was hardly acting in an adult manner.

'Congratulations,' she murmured. 'I had no idea Mr Piace was engaged.'

'It's not official,' Rebecca backtracked, sounding less confident, 'but it's understood. We are going to get engaged on my twenty-first birthday and we have Nonno's blessing.'

The sound of slow footsteps drew May's attention to the path leading down to the balustrade.

'Nonno.' Rebecca's sulky expression melted into a smile. 'You must not tire yourself out.'

'Thank you, Rebecca. When I want your assistance I will ask for it.'

May expected Rebecca to flare up at the reprimand but after another venomous glance in May's direction she lowered her eyes and moved to one side allowing Auguste Lombardi to pass.

'Miss Maxwell.' He turned his attention to May. 'I'm sorry if I wasn't as welcoming as I should have been earlier. I find parties tiring these days.'

'I understand,' May replied. 'I'm not too good at this sort of thing, either. Though it's a lovely party.'

'There's no need to be economical with the truth.' His eyes twinkled. 'You are out of your comfort zone.'

'There are a lot of guests,' May acknowledged, 'and I don't know anyone here.'

'And this party has been too much for you.' Rebecca elbowed her way back into the conversation. 'Why don't I take you back inside, Nonno, where you can rest?'

'Thank you,' he acknowledged. 'Ms Maxwell, if you would excuse us.'

May watched him lean heavily on Rebecca's shoulder as she led him back towards the villa. Deciding to follow their example, May headed for the sanctuary of the studio. It was still early but as the host had already departed she decided it couldn't be regarded as bad manners if she did the same.

'You are leaving?' Vin accosted her as she reached the camellia garden.

'I've had a long day,' May replied.

'And you have another long one tomorrow.'

'Do I?'

'I'll pick you up at nine o'clock.'

'Where are we going?'

'To the circuit.'

'Fitness training?'

'No. The autodromo is for cars.'

May recalled Betta saying the Lombardi fortune had been something to do with motor racing.

'Wear comfortable clothes,' Vin advised

as they reached the door of May's studio. 'The autodromo is not for sandals.'

'They're not mine.' May spoke without thinking.

'I didn't think they were. If your Limester is anything like my home village, designer dresses are rare.'

Vin's tie had now given up the battle with his collar and he had even undone the top button of his shirt, May presumed in an attempt to ease his discomfort.

'You're leaving the party, too?'

'I have done my duty. The diehards will probably remain until the small hours. I hope they won't keep you awake.'

May stifled a yawn behind her hand.

'On location you get used to unsocial hours. I won't have any trouble falling asleep. By the way,' May turned back from the studio door opened by one of the maids who had been waiting up to welcome her back, 'congratulations on your forthcoming engagement.'

'I wasn't aware I was engaged.' Vin looked surprised. 'But when I am I will let you know about it. '

A Friendly Face

The Hector Lombardi Autodromo, named after Auguste's son, was built on the site of an old aerodrome, a short drive from the villa.

'It started from humble beginnings.' Vin continued his explanation as he and May sat in his office above the workshops overlooking the circuit. 'But such was the popularity of our venue we soon outgrew our premises and a few years ago the unit was completely rebuilt.

'In the past Sr Lombardi has been very generous with his time but these days he prefers to take life a little easier, which leaves me to look after the daily running of the autodromo. So now you know what I do for a living and why I have dirt under my fingernails.'

In the background May could hear the rev of exhausts and static announcements from an overhead speaker giving out statistics as drivers completed their trials. A high-octane smell of fuel lingered in the air and the buzz of activity from the forecourt below Vin's office indicated a bustling and successful business.

Vin was dressed down in a dark blue boiler suit and he had nodded approval on seeing May's choice of dress — cut off jeans, an oversized sweatshirt and a jumper slung carelessly around her shoulders. Away from the villa and in the less sophisticated atmosphere of the autodromo May felt more relaxed and Vin she sensed felt the same. As he opened up to her she was sure this was where his passion lay, not with the jet-set lazing by the water, gossiping about the latest scandal to hit their exclusive group.

'Sr Lombardi wanted to set up an academy where young people could safely sharpen up on their driving skills,' Vin continued. 'Too often we read of accidents that could so easily have been avoided if the driver had paid a little more attention to road safety or had the knowledge to do so.'

'And he named the circuit after his son?'

'Yes.'

'After he died in an accident?'

'Not something we talk about,' Vin replied, leaving May with the feeling she had been rebuked.

She wished she could explain the real reason why she had asked her question. It wasn't vulgar curiosity but the need to know her mother's connection with the family. Had she and Hector been an item?

Was Hector the reason she had fled Italy never to return and why she would never talk about her time here?

'Cars these days are much more powerful than they used to be and young men . . . ' Vin paused. 'I am not being sexist but fast driving tends to favour young men and they want to show off skills they don't have.

'They need to develop a feel for the road and the car they are driving. Every year we award a prestigious trophy for the best performance. It is heavily contested and the event is always over subscribed.

'As well as the Lombardi cup there is a personal introduction to Sr Lombardi and a test drive in a formula racing car.'

'Is this where you learned to drive?' May ventured a question she hoped wouldn't provoke another rebuke.

'We are not a driving school, we do not give lessons,' Vin corrected her. May stifled another sigh. Another black mark and she hadn't been here over an hour. 'I learned to drive on my father's motorbike. I took my full driving test when I was eighteen.'

'Did you pass first time?' May tried another question hoping this wouldn't backfire on her.

'I did.'

'Lucky you.' May did nothing to disguise her envy. Vin looked up from the statistics he was studying.

'You had a bad experience learning to drive?'

'It took me five attempts to pass my

test,' May said, 'And when I finally did pass I'm sure the instructor took pity on me because it was snowing.'

'You took your test in the snow?' Vin's eyes betrayed his surprise and not a little admiration.

'I backed into a block of ice,' May laughed at the memory, 'and the instructor said I was lucky because it stopped me from hitting the pavement when I was doing my three point turn.'

'Snow is not a problem from which we suffer in Bella Acqua.'

May relaxed. Vin was actually being pleasant to her. With him in a good mood she might be able to tap him for more information about the Lombardis.

'Perhaps we can offer you a job here, driving in extreme conditions. We can't simulate snow but we do have a rain machine and a skid pan.'

'I don't know how long I will be staying.' May was quick to react.

'I was forgetting.' Vin looked serious again. 'You are on a mission.'

'You must see I can't abuse Sr

Lombardi's hospitality for ever.'

Vin eyed the tower of paperwork threatening to topple over on to his desk.

'You could abuse it a little longer if you were prepared to tackle the filing.'

'Not one of my skills,' May admitted, wishing she had paid more attention to the business studies course she had been forced to attend after she left sixth form college.

'There's no money to send you to Bali on a gap year so it's no use asking,' her grandmother had informed her when several of her college friends had been arranging a trip.

'I'll ask Tish for the money.' May relived the painful scene in her head. 'She's not mean.'

Coco had looked unusually upset.

'I wish we had the money, darling, but we don't.'

At this point, Zeph, her grandfather had intervened. Rudeness to Coco was something he would not allow under any circumstances. As a punishment May had been enrolled for a business studies course but after one term all parties involved admitted it had been a mistake and May had been allowed to change to her first love — drama.

'Office work and I don't get along,' May informed Vin, 'so unless you never want to find anything again, the filing is better left where it is.'

'A pity.' Vin shrugged. 'Rebecca was supposed to have a stab at it but I dare say I'll get around to it one day. Er, where was I?' Vin asked with a distracted frown.

'Driving skills?' May suggested.

'Right.' Vin elbowed the filing out of his eye line. 'My duties also include heading up the team responsible for making sure we don't infringe any regulations. It's a constant headache, far worse than the filing.'

May's eyes strayed to the bright sunshine beating through the skylight, signifying another warm day.

'You are restless?' May was about to deny she was any such thing when Vin spoke again. 'I agree it's far too good a day to be stuck indoors. Would you like to look round outside? It's this way.'

A red-haired woman strode towards them from the direction of the work-shops as they emerged into the sunlight. She too was dressed in the uniform boiler suit displaying the distinctive Lombardi dragon logo.

'There you are,' she greeted Vin. 'I was starting to think you had overslept after the party.'

'I didn't stay late.'

'You never do,' she complained, turning to May. 'And who is this?'

'May Maxwell. May, meet Florence Amaria.'

Florence's face lit up as Vin performed the introduction and with her arms extended she embraced May so fiercely she could hardly breathe.

'My love,' she kissed her on both cheeks, 'you are so beautiful. Do you not think so, Vin?'

May's face flamed.

'I hope,' Vin said in a voice betraying no emotion, 'Florence's welcome has made up for the coolness of the reception you have received from everybody else at the Villa Lombardi.'

As Florence released her May recognised she was the woman who had driven her car through the villa gates two days ago while she had been concealed behind the statue.

Florence made a gesture of irritation. 'The autodromo is a male environment. It's nice to have another female to talk to. Motorcars and racing are very macho symbols, especially to Italian men.' She turned back to May. 'I am the Lombardi symbol of modernity. I am allowed to drive any vehicle I like in the interests of feminine equality,' she boasted. 'I bet Vin did not tell you that.'

'No, he didn't.'

May's reply seemed to please Florence.

'I thought not. What have you got to say for yourself, Vin Piace?'

'You don't need me to tell anyone you are a very good and safe driver.'

'Carry on.' Florence winked at May. 'I like what I am hearing.'

'Andreas, Florence's husband, was our chief engineer. Florence used to drive him to the autodromo every day.'

'My Andreas had motor oil in his veins,' Florence added with a proud toss of her red hair.

'Florence sort of stayed on after she was widowed,' Vin continued. 'No-one has summoned up enough courage to send her away.'

Florence made another disparaging noise at the back of her throat.

'The young mechanics, they like me. I am their Mama In Loco Parentis,' she laughed again. 'But enough about cars, my beautiful May, why did I not see you at the party last night?'

'I was there.'

'Why did you not come and talk to me?'

'I talked to Rebecca.'

'You haven't answered my question,' Florence said with a stern frown.

'I wouldn't have known who you were. There were so many people around.'

'Nonsense, everyone knows me, don't

they, Vin?'

'Stop showing off, Florence. You're not world famous. There are still one or two people left on the planet who are not aware of your existence.'

'May Maxwell, you say?' Florence put a thoughtful finger to her lips. 'I don't remember seeing the name on the invitation list.'

'You don't remember it because . . . ' Vin tried to interrupt.

'But why do I feel we've already met?' Florence brushed aside his attempt to provide an explanation and looked hard at May.

'If you'd let me explain . . . ' Vin raised his voice.

'Explanations will have to wait,' Florence rammed her safety helmet back on to her head, 'I'm needed in the pit for a test drive. I will talk to you later, my beautiful May.'

'If you're not too exhausted by whirlwind Florence shall we continue with our tour?' Vin invited after Florence headed off for the pit lane.

'Florence is Rebecca's mother, isn't she?'

'Yes.'

'And Florence issued the invitations for the party?'

'The celebrations were all her idea. You may have noticed Florence gets things done and no-one dares say no to her, not even Sr Lombardi. Now, enough about Florence. Pollution . . . 'Vin led May towards another workshop.

'Every day we are developing new systems and introducing measures to minimise the impact our little circuit has on the environment, but the car is here to stay, unless we decide to go back to chariots. Are you listening to me?' Vin gave a wry smile. 'I know waste products aren't the most riveting topic of conversation but it is important.'

'Who gave Florence the list of people to invite to the party?'

Vin sighed.

'I don't know.'

'Was it Sr Lombardi?'

'You can ask him yourself this

61

afternoon.'

   'This afternoon?'

   'He has invited you to tea.'

Tea for Two

The windows in the high ceilinged drawing-room overlooked the lake, letting in a cool afternoon breeze. The room, a fine example of the Baroque period of architecture, was exquisitely furnished. In a far corner May noticed a harpsichord and remembered reading how music had played a significant role in the fashions of the time.

Her footsteps echoed over the floorboards as she walked towards Sr Lombardi. To May's consternation there appeared to be no other guests. Two menservants were bustling discreetly around a low table setting it for a traditional English tea, their every move supervised by Sr Lombardi.

'There you are,' he greeted May. 'I trust you will forgive me if I don't stand up. I was taught a gentleman always stands to greet a lady but today my legs do not want to obey the commands of my brain.'

It was easy to smile at such a charming man. Despite his advanced years it was obvious Auguste Lombardi still took great care over his appearance.

'Please, sit down.' He gestured towards a padded seat. 'You may go. We will serve ourselves. Thank you,' he said, dismissing the two menservants.

'I was expecting a party.' May looked round the room.

'We are having a party, aren't we? Tea for two, like the song.' The dent in the centre of his chin deepened as he smiled at her.

'I suppose we are,' she agreed and sitting down tried to relax.

Ever since Vin had broken the news of Auguste's invitation she had been on tenterhooks. She was convinced Sr Lombardi held the key to her past and that was why she had wanted this interview but now the moment was here she realised how ill prepared she was. She didn't have a plan or any idea how to approach the delicate subject of her mother's possible relationship with his son.

'You are comfortable in the studio?' he asked as May passed him a cup of Earl Grey.

'Very. Thank you. It was most kind of you to offer it to me.' May felt like a character in an afternoon matinee making polite drawing-room conversation. 'And is it you I have to thank for the dress, too, and the sandals?'

Auguste looked blank.

'I know nothing about such things. My housekeeper takes care of my guests' needs. I am glad you liked them.'

Auguste was dressed in a crisp white shirt open at the neck and charcoal grey slacks with razor sharp creases.

'I have been hearing about your attempts to gain admittance to the villa.' He spoke slowly and carefully. Auguste raised a hand to silence May as she attempted to interrupt. 'You have tenacity, a quality I admire and respect. I understand you took on one of my security guards?'

'And lost,' May admitted. 'He wouldn't let me in.'

'Quite right and proper, but now you are here, please have a cucumber sandwich. See, the crusts have been cut off and they are on white bread in the traditional English style.'

May dutifully helped herself to a sandwich.

'Talking of the studio,' Auguste stirred his tea, 'history has it Napoleon Bonaparte slept there.'

'In the studio?' May dropped her sandwich on to her plate.

'There are many such stories about the villa. I do not question them — I merely tell them to my guests to break the ice. It usually works.' He leaned forward and placed a sandwich on his own plate. 'However, I can assure you the frescoes in this room are genuine.'

May looked up at the ceiling.

'They are beautiful,' she agreed.

'Have we met before?' Auguste enquired. Although it was a seemingly innocent question, May suspected it was

66

a loaded one and she needed to choose her words carefully.

'No, we haven't.' She coughed and swallowed the last of her cucumber sandwich.

'I don't go out much these days so I don't meet many new people. I think I would have remembered if a beautiful young lady had crossed my path, but there is something . . . ' He shook his head. 'Take no notice.'

A rush of colour to her face caused May to feel uncomfortably hot.

'I think you'll find you're not allowed to say such things in the present day and age, Sr Lombardi.' May wished he wouldn't look at her quite so intently.

'You must call me Auguste,' he insisted, 'and I apologise if I have been over familiar. I come from a generation when flattery was deemed a compliment, not a crime against the female sex.'

May suspected in his day Auguste had been a bit of a rogue. She didn't doubt he used the same chat-up lines on all his female guests.

'You are smiling, good. Perhaps you would do me the kindness of pouring me another cup of tea before we get down to business. Have you had sufficient to eat?'

Assuring him she had, May leaned back in her padded chair and did her best to remain confident.

'Is this your first trip to my country?'

'I was born in Milan,' May replied.

'Is your mother Italian?'

'No, she is English.'

'At the risk of sounding inquisitive, what was she doing in Italy?'

'I don't know.'

'And your father — what can you tell me about him?'

May looked down at her hands, uncertain how to respond.

'Nothing,' she admitted in a quiet voice.

'We seem to have drawn a blank, don't we?'

Auguste sounded sympathetic for which May was relieved. She had half expected him to call the two men-servants back and have her escorted off the premises.

'Tell me about yourself,' he invited.

'I'm an actress,' May replied.

'I suspected something of the sort.'

'Did you?'

'From the way you crossed the room. There are few people who can carry off such an entrance with style.'

'Did you set me a test?' May demanded.

'Guilty,' Auguste replied. 'My dear May — I may call you by your first name?'

'Yes, of course.'

'You can't blame me for being intrigued by your presence here. Most of my birthday guests are extremely tedious and have limited conversational skills. When I am told a young English woman has tried to gain access to the villa and is prepared to assume a false identity in order to do so you can appreciate my position. I am intrigued. I see you as a challenge and I don't know about you but I am enjoying myself.'

A butterfly fluttered through the open window, landed on one of the curtains, flapped its wings then flew off again.

'Are you enjoying yourself?' Auguste asked.

May nodded.

'I am enjoying my tea. Thank you.'

'My pleasure, and I insist you stay until you have sorted out the gaps in your mother's life, the real reason for your visit. I am right, aren't I?' May realised it would not do to underestimate Auguste Lombardi. He was nobody's fool. 'I presume your mother is not with you.'

'No.'

'And was it her invitation you used in your attempts to gain admittance to the villa?'

'Yes.'

'Very resourceful of you.'

'Do you know why my mother was invited to your birthday celebrations?'

'You will have to take up matters of that nature with Florence.' Auguste dismissed the question as it were of little importance. 'I was not involved in any of the arrangements.' May lapsed into silence. 'Might I enquire what your

70

mother thought of the subterfuge and why she didn't come to the party with you?'

'She's on her way to Australia with my grandmother.'

'I see.'

'She is entertainments manager for a cruise company and they are going to visit a friend of my grandmother's in Melbourne.'

'And are you married?' Auguste asked. 'You must forgive the questions. If you feel I am being too nosy tell me to stop.'

'I am not married.' May glanced down to a faded head and shoulders photo on a side table. 'Was this your wife?' she asked in a soft voice.

A look of intense sadness crossed Auguste's face.

'She was so beautiful.' His voice was a husky croak. 'My Giovanna.'

The sound of a door banging open broke the silence. Rebecca whirled into the room.

'Nonno,' she berated Auguste. 'What are you doing?'

'I am having tea with my charming companion, May.' Although he spoke politely to Rebecca, May sensed he was annoyed by the interruption.

'I'd like a cup, too.' She clicked her fingers and indicated to May that she was to pour one out for her. 'No milk and a slice of lemon.'

'Really, Rebecca, if you would like a cup of tea you must serve yourself. May is my guest.'

Rebecca thumped the teapot back down on the tray with a sulky pout and reaching out, grabbed a slice of apricot sponge off the cake stand. Not bothering with a plate or one of the laundered linen serviettes provided she crammed the cake into her mouth in two bites.

'Rebecca addresses me as her nonno,' Auguste explained, 'but she is not my granddaughter and I am not her grandfather. Alas, I have no grandchildren — a cause of great regret to me.'

'My mother told me you were down at the autodromo this morning.' Rebecca commenced another verbal attack on

May.

'Vin drove me down.'

'What did you think of it?' Auguste enquired.

'I could see you have invested a lot of time and money to make it a thriving business,' May replied.

'It has been my life's work.' Auguste sounded tired. 'If I have saved one young life then it has been successful.'

'What's your interest in the autodromo?' Rebecca demanded, still glaring at May.

'I don't have one.'

'Why are you here? Has she told you, Nonno, Vin caught her prowling around outside the villa gates? She was up to no good, yet here she is having tea with you. You are far too trusting.'

'Please, I would like to rest.' Auguste briefly closed his eyes. 'Perhaps you would leave?'

'You've tired him out,' Rebecca hissed, manhandling May out of the room.

'I did no such thing,' May objected.

'Next time you are asked to tea, run it

past me or my mother first. No-one gets to see Nonno without our say so.'

With an ugly look on her face Rebecca stalked away.

So Many Questions

Back in her studio May saw another dress, bag and accessories had been placed on her bed. The latest programme of activities on her bedside table indicated more guests were due to arrive for an evening concert of classical music. She toyed briefly with the idea of deserting the villa and heading home. She had made little headway with her investigations and her presence was clearly unsettling Rebecca.

She sat on the bed for a moment and tried to gather her thoughts.

Auguste had shown her nothing but kindness and May's conscience told her it would be unfair to him and discourteous in the extreme to disappear without a word, but his questions about her past had deepened her suspicions.

She was convinced something had happened here and that was the reason she had been born in Milan, but several other questions remained unanswered.

Who was her father? What was Florence's connection to Tish? Why would her mother never talk about her past? What could she be hiding?

May's fingers brushed against the material of the midnight blue crushed satin dress. Another more uncomfortable suspicion was beginning to form at the back of her mind. Did Auguste suspect his son Hector was her father? If so, Auguste was her grandfather, which could be a difficult situation in the making.

As she was applying her make-up there was a light tap on the door.

'I thought you might like a glass of this.' Florence held up a bottle of wine and two glasses. 'Can I come in?' Taking May's surprised silence for assent she eased past her.

'We can have a gossip while you're getting ready for the concert. I'll sit down here and I promise not to be a nuisance. If you'd rather I went away don't hesitate to say. I have broad shoulders.'

'I could do with some company,' May admitted.

'Was tea with Auguste an ordeal?' Florence pulled a sympathetic face.

'No, he was charming.'

'Are you up to telling me what's given you a face like one of your damp English afternoons?' A dimple tugged at the corner of Florence's generous mouth.

'I suppose Auguste made me feel bad. I mean, I am here under false pretences.'

'Yes, you are. You tried to sneak into the celebrations clutching Tish Delacourt's invitation, didn't you?'

'Yes.'

'Was this with her approval?'

'No,' May admitted.

'You mean you stole her invitation?'

'Yes and no.'

'A good answer, I must use it next time I am in a tight corner.'

'Tish is my mother.' May closed her eyes and waited for the fallout.

'I knew it.' Florence leaped to her feet. 'This calls for a big hug. I should have guessed you were Tish's daughter. You have the same colour of eyes.'

When Florence had finished kissing May on both cheeks she collapsed back down into her chair and took a large gulp of her wine.

'Where is Tish?' she demanded.

'She doesn't know about the party and she doesn't know I'm here.' May fiddled with her hairbrush.

'Right,' Florence acknowledged with a slow smile. 'You still haven't answered my question. Where is she?'

'On a cruise with my grandmother.'

'Here, let me.' Florence grabbed the brush from May and eased her hair away from her face. 'What beautiful earrings.'

She fingered one of them. 'They were a present from my mother.'

'Quite lovely,' Florence said before vigorously brushing May's hair. 'I used to brush Rebecca's hair when she was a little girl but she won't let me near it now. It's all part of the growing up process, I suppose. Do you have children?' she asked.

'I'm not married,' May replied.

'Doesn't seem to make a difference these days,' Florence remarked. 'What do you think of Vin Piace?'

'Rebecca's fiancé?'

'Who told you they were engaged?'

'Rebecca.'

'The little minx.' Florence smiled. 'She's always had a crush on poor old Vin, but he's years older than her. I can assure you there is no arranged marriage, so that leaves the field free for you.'

'Sorry?' May paused, her lipstick in her hand.

'You and Vin, you'd be perfect for each other.'

'You didn't come here to talk about me and Vin.' May recapped her lipstick with a firm twist, noting her heightened colour in the mirror.

'Actually I didn't,' Florence looked less sure of herself. 'I've got zillions of questions I want to ask you but I don't know where to start and I'm scared you might think I'm being rude.'

'Can I ask you some questions?'

'Good idea. Fire away.'

'You knew my mother in the past?'

'Yes, the three of us used to go around together all the time.'

'There were three of you?'

'Did your mother not mention Lis Gilbert?' Florence looked flustered.

May shook her head.

'I know nothing of my mother's past. She would never talk about it.'

'The past is another country to some people.' Florence lapsed into silence.

'Is there anything you can tell me about my mother?'

'I suppose it wouldn't do any harm.'

May clenched her fists, resisting the urge to tell Florence to stop playing hard to get.

After a few moments' thought, Florence spoke.

'Tish and Lis were a singing duo. They used to work the private party scene. They went to all the best places and mixed with the rich and famous. They called themselves I Bei Gemelli. The Beautiful Twins. Of course they weren't twins but they were beautiful.'

'Did you sing, too?' May asked.

'Me? Goodness — I can't sing a note.'

'How did you meet them?'

'I always loved cars. One day their driver let them down. I stepped in and soon the arrangement became permanent. We went everywhere together. I did all their driving and I have to say it was a challenge.

'You would not believe the amount of luggage they had — equipment, costumes and personal belongings. They had the loan of a van but it was always breaking down because no-one had any money to get it properly repaired.

'There were lots of people, mostly young men — sort of self-appointed roadies — who were more than willing to help us. They made life much easier. Did I say something funny?' she demanded.

'The idea of you acting as nursemaid to my mother somehow doesn't seem real.'

'You don't know the half of it.' Florence warmed to her tale. 'In those days I had flaming red hair, Tish had flowing chestnut hair and Lis . . . ' Florence sighed and paused in her hair brushing.

'What about Lis?' May asked.

'She was a natural blonde. Her father was Norwegian and her mother Italian. It was an exotic combination. Men would fall over themselves to help us out when things went wrong and Lis wasn't above using her personal attributes to get us out of a fix.

'It worked every time. The same bunch of guys seemed to follow us around and I'm sure it was because she was so beautiful.'

'What happened to Lis?'

'I met Andreas and,' an expression May did not understand crossed Florence's face, 'we split up. It was all rather sudden really, but we were young and still making our lives. Life draws you in different directions when you are young. Things happen then they can't be undone.'

'Why do you think my mother doesn't ever talk about her past?' May continued, intrigued.

'I don't know. Your mother didn't want to keep in touch with her old friends. Some people don't.'

'And Lis?' May prompted.

'She married well. No surprises there. She was always ambitious. She wasn't going to marry a garage mechanic. So,' Florence laid the hairbrush down on the dressing table, 'there you have it.'

'Why did you contact my mother after so many years?'

'She wrote a letter of condolence when my Andreas died.' Florence lost some of her exuberance. 'I don't know how she found out but my world fell apart and I didn't reply to her letter — something I later regretted.

'When I decided to arrange the eight-ieth birthday celebrations for Auguste I sent an invitation to the address she had put on the envelope. I wasn't even sure she still lived there. I am so glad you responded. It is wonderful to see you and somehow it makes everything right.'

May was left wondering what had really gone wrong between the girls to cause such a rift when there was another knock at the door.

'The guests have started to arrive.' Vin was outside. 'And Auguste is looking for you, Florence.'

'I must go and greet everyone.' Florence sounded relieved that Vin had interrupted them. He ambled into the studio. His bow tie was again crooked and with a sigh of impatience May stood up.

'Come here,' she said.

'Why?' A faint look of alarm crossed Vin's face.

'Because,' with a few deft movements of her fingers May straightened his collar and adjusted the wings of his tie, 'it needed help.'

She stepped back to admire her handiwork. Mingled with the smell of shower gel was the ever-present faint aroma of motor oil.

'We had a last minute emergency at the autodromo and I dressed in a hurry, thank you.' Vin eased his tie into a more comfortable position. 'What was Florence doing here?' he asked.

'Amongst other things, dispensing wine. Would you like a glass?' May indicated the bottle and turned back to her dressing table mirror.

'I'm not used to this sort of thing.' Vin perched uncomfortably on a dress stool.

'Parties or watching a female finish her make-up?' May glanced over her shoulder before taking pity on his discomfort. 'I won't be long.'

'Both, really,' Vin responded.

'Then let me distract you.'

'I think perhaps we had better be going.' Vin jumped to his feet in his hurry to leave.

'Florence and Auguste.' May rubbed a discreet drop of perfume on to her wrists and massaged the remainder into the base of her neck.

'What about them?'

'Are they an item?'

'Not in the way you mean.'

'How do you know what I mean?' May teased Vin, looking at him over the rim of her glass.

'You are asking if they are lovers.'

She spluttered into her wine.

'I suppose that was rather obvious,' she admitted, wiping her lips with a tissue, 'and you don't have to answer. I'm merely trying to get my head round things and it isn't easy.'

The expression on Vin's face softened.

'I can tell you the relationship between Florence and Auguste suits them both. Andreas's death left a big hole in everyone's lives and Florence turned to Auguste for comfort. He looked after her and Rebecca, as we all did.'

'Thank you for that,' May replied.

'Do you have any other questions?' he asked.

'I do have one.' May came to a decision.

'Yes?' The wary look replaced Vin's smile.

'When am I free to leave?'

'You don't want to stay on?'

'I'm beginning to think some secrets should remain hidden. My mother must have had a good reason for not telling

86

me about her past and I have to respect her decision.'

'I don't agree.'

'You must realise by now I am not here to steal the family silver or to kidnap Sr Lombardi.'

'I don't think I really believed that was your aim in the first place but I was intrigued as to what you were up to.'

'I've told Florence Tish Delacourt is my mother and the reason I decided to attend the party was as family representative. So everyone now knows who I am and why I am here.'

Vin paced the carpet, a thoughtful frown wrinkling his forehead.

'All the same, my decision still stands.'

'What decision?'

'That you will stay on.'

'Aren't you rather overstepping your authority? You have no right to detain me.' May now wished she had taken the opportunity to tighten Vin's tie and not straighten it.

'I am Sr Lombardi's right-hand man.'

'At the autodromo. Here at the villa

you're a guest like everyone else.'

'As you say,' he acknowledged.

'May I ask why you are trying to stop me from leaving?'

'Because of your earrings.'

'I beg your pardon? What have my earrings got to do with anything?'

'I want to know why you are wearing vintage anemone emeralds surrounded by brilliant cut diamonds.'

'Would you mind repeating that?' May gasped.

'I suspect they are part of the famous Lombardi collection and I'm sure I'm not the only one who would like to know what they are doing in your possession.'

False Accusations

'How dare you?' May stepped back, her eyes burning with anger.

'How dare I what?' Vin looked perplexed.

'Accuse me of theft.'

'I'm not!' Vin protested.

'You said . . . ' May began, but Vin interrupted.

'The Lombardi emeralds went missing years ago. Out of the blue you turn up and try to bluff your way into Auguste Lombardi's eightieth birthday brunch. The next evening you are seen wearing the missing emeralds to his party. You have to admit it looks suspicious.'

'What makes you such an expert on vintage jewellery?'

'I know the real thing when I see it and I have seen pictures of the missing emeralds.'

'This time you are wrong. My earrings are costume. They are coloured glass.'

'How can you be certain?'

May floundered for an explanation. The diamonds sparkled back at her in the mirror.

'My mother gave them to me,' she finished in a lame voice. Vin lowered his eyes as if reluctant to display his disbelief. 'Anyway, how can you be certain they are the real thing?'

Vin glanced at his watch with a worried frown.

'I spoke out of turn. I'm sorry. We'll talk later.'

'We'll talk now,' May insisted.

A powdered footman announced his arrival with a discreet cough.

'Signor? Signorina?'

'Yes, we're coming. Please,' Vin turned back to May, 'don't mention any of this to Auguste,' he implored. 'It would upset him.'

May swallowed to ease the dryness in her mouth.

'The reason I came to Bella Acqua was to find out what happened here with my mother,' she said in a softer voice. 'I'm not a thief and neither is Tish.'

'We'll sort it out.' Vin gave her arm a comforting squeeze. 'I'm on your side and it would do no good upsetting Auguste's birthday celebrations by making a scene, would it?'

May was forced to give a reluctant nod of her head.

'I won't say anything,' she promised.

'And I'll do all I can to help you solve your mystery — so, friends?'

'As long as there are no more accusations about me or members of my family being crooks.'

'There won't be.' Vin raised her hand to his lips. 'There. Sealed with a kiss.' May stiffened and Vin took a step backwards. 'You're not going to rage at me for making a gesture of friendship, are you?'

May extricated her hand from Vin's.

'No.'

'Good, now if we delay any longer Auguste will think we're not coming.'

May followed Vin outside to where the footman was waiting for them. He held his lighted candelabra aloft.

'Please take care. The ground is un-even in places.'

As they made their way through the camellia-scented gardens towards the muted chatter of the guests already assembled on the terrace, May was unable to dispel thoughts of her earrings.

There was no way Tish could have afforded genuine emeralds. Could they possibly be real? Even with her prestigious job May knew her mother's salary would not run to brilliant cut diamonds. So where had they come from? 'Signorina Maxwell is sitting here.' The footman indicated a seat in the front row and removed the card attached to the padded velvet cushion.

May was relieved to see Vin was not occupying the adjacent seat. The thought of sitting beside him for two long hours and with no means of escape was not a prospect she would have relished. She needed to focus on her mother's past and distractions like Vin Piace promising to help and kissing her hand would get in the way.

'What a treat,' May's neighbour greeted her, politely standing up until she was settled in her seat before returning his attention to the programme.

'I see we have a Mozart sonata scheduled, as well as a violin solo and a piano recital, all wonderful choices. Franco Napoli,' he introduced himself, 'and my wife Sofia.'

'Ms Maxwell and I have already met.' Seated on the far side of her husband, Sofia acknowledged May with a gracious nod.

'You have?' Franco turned to his wife. 'When?'

'At the party the other night, we had a little chat down by the water and,' Sofia leaned forward, 'perhaps in the interval we could get to know each other better?'

'Excellent suggestion,' Franco agreed. 'You will join us for a drink, Ms Maxwell?'

'Thank you.' May was glad to have a further chance of avoiding Vin's company during the interval.

Franco glanced across to the stage as a hush went round the audience.

'Here they come,' he announced as the musicians' arrival was greeted with a polite smattering of applause.

The night air was balmy and May allowed the gentle notes of the music to soothe her troubled mind. The velvet sky was studded with stars twinkling like the diamonds in her earrings.

Franco Napoli looked at her in concern as her sigh came out as a gentle moan.

'You are unwell?' he whispered.

'The music,' May improvised. 'Sorry.'

'It evokes many memories,' Franco agreed, offering her the use of his linen handkerchief. 'Will this help?'

May took it with a gesture of thanks and turned her attention back to the concert.

'Time for some refreshment, I think.' Franco gave her a polite nudge as the musicians left the stage. 'You were lost in the moment?' he enquired with his kindly smile.

'Something got to me,' May said by way of explanation. 'And it's such a beautiful evening.'

'Franco, my love,' Sofia removed a speck of dust from the collar of his jacket, 'I speak better English than you and I know you are itching to talk to your business acquaintances so why don't you get Ms Maxwell and I a drink before you join your friends?'

'Ms Maxwell?' Franco enquired with a roguish smile. 'Could you possibly live without my company for a quarter of an hour?'

'She could,' Sofia intervened, 'if you bring our promised drinks.'

'Pronto, my love.' Franco bustled away.

'Shall we sit under the trees where no-one will spot us?' Sofia urged May towards some garden furniture. 'And you can tell me the real reason why you were sighing so dramatically.'

'I wouldn't want to keep you from your husband or your friends.'

'I am afraid there are few people here I

would count as true friends.' Sofia made a face. 'I have never blended in with the party set and I am sure the sole reason they tolerate me is because I am married to one of the most influential men in Bella Acqua.'

'I see.'

'There is no need to look so shocked, darling. I love my Franco to bits but I am under no illusion. Many people thought I married him to gain respectability.'

'I'm sure it's not true.'

'I have a past,' Sofia confided with a wink, 'but let's not waste time talking about other people. I want to know about you. Thank you, my darling.' Sofia accepted the drinks from a hovering Franco. 'You will come back for us at the end of the interval, won't you?'

'How could I forget to escort two beautiful ladies back to their seats? I shall be the envy of all the men present.'

'Isn't he a poppet?' Sofia smiled indulgently at her gallant husband. 'Now,' she turned to May, 'tell me everything.'

'I don't know what you mean.'

'Gossip is rife. Everyone wants to know who you are and why you are occupying Auguste's studio. It is quite an honour, you know.'

'What are people saying about me?' May asked in a shocked voice.

'You don't want to know. What people don't know they make up and I wouldn't like to repeat some of the stories I heard — and before you accuse me of scandal-mongering I have to say I know you are Tish Delacourt's daughter. I am right, aren't I?'

'How did you find out?'

'My darling girl,' her words echoed those of Florence's, 'I suspected it was so when I first met you, but to answer your question, Rebecca was broadcasting what happened, about how you had used someone else's invitation in an attempt to gain access to the villa.

'It wasn't difficult to find out who she was talking about. How that little troublemaker can be Florence's daughter I do not understand. Her father Andreas was a perfect gentleman. She doesn't take after either of her parents.'

'You knew Andreas?'

'Hmm.' Sofia gave a reluctant nod.

'Did you know my mother?'

A smile of pure happiness spread across Sofia's face.

'She was one of the beautiful twins.'

'So Florence tells me.'

'They had quite a reputation, those girls. Florence was their driver and she used to chauffeur them around from gig to gig.'

'One last gig . . . ' May repeated thoughtfully.

'I beg your pardon?'

'Florence wrote it on my mother's invitation.'

'The girls had their last gig a long time ago,' Sofia said in a thoughtful voice.

'Can you tell me anything about the Beautiful Twins?' May asked.

'What exactly do you know about them?'

'Nothing, really.'

'Did your mother never mention them?'

'No.'

'But I suspect something else is worrying you?' Sofia narrowed her eyes in speculation.

'I have learned the earrings I am wearing are worth a lot of money but when my mother gave them to me she led me to believe they were costume jewellery.'

'And you are upset by this?'

'There are so many gaps in my mother's life I feel,' May shrugged, 'something's missing in my life, too.'

'It is no wonder you are sad.'

May glanced at Sofia's profile as she gazed across the gardens. In her youth she must have been very beautiful, May thought, as Sofia fiddled nervously with the fine gold neck chain she was wearing.

'Having been the subject of gossip when I married my Franco,' Sofia spoke slowly, 'I do not like to talk about others behind their back but I will tell you a story and you must make your own conclusions.'

'I'm good with that,' May agreed.

'Many years ago there was a spate of

high-profile jewels robberies in this area. Frequently after the Beautiful Twins had performed at one of their villa parties, jewellery would disappear.

'It happened too often for it to be considered pure chance. There had to be a connection.'

May swallowed the lump of apprehension rising in her throat.

'Were the culprits caught?'

In the distance a bell rang, signifying the second half of the concert was due to start in five minutes.

'You know Sr Lombardi had a son, Hector?'

'Yes.'

'And you also know he died?'

'In a car accident.'

'The robberies stopped almost immediately after his death.'

'Hector was involved?'

'I do not know. Out of respect to Hector's father, enquiries were scaled down.' Sofia stood up. 'Here comes Franco.'

May's legs were shaking as she stood up.

'Do you think my mother was involved?'

Sofia looked at May then gently stroked her face.

'Your mother was a wonderful person who never did a dishonest thing in her life.' Her eyes softened. 'If you want to know more about what happened why don't you ask Vin Piace?'

'What would Vin know about the robberies?'

'His father, Alberto, was the chief policeman leading the investigation team.'

Follow Your Dreams

'You are here to escort Ms Maxwell to the buffet?' Franco greeted Vin as he approached their small group at the end of the concert. 'I would ask you to join us but my wife and I are guests of one of my business acquaintances.'

Sofia kissed May on the cheek.

'I have no doubt we shall meet up again soon.' She smiled. 'Our destinies are entwined. Now remember,' she added, 'follow your dreams.'

With a coquettish smile at Vin, Sofia linked her arm through her husband's.

'Come along, Franco, it doesn't do to keep important people waiting.'

'I'm not hungry. I'm going back to the studio.' May could barely summon up the manners to speak politely to Vin. She was still reeling from the shock of learning about his father.

'Good idea. We'll have a late supper sent across.'

'Alone,' she added.

'For two,' Vin insisted.

May turned on her heel, hoping to outpace Vin, but she was not used to walking in high-heeled sandals and Vin had no difficulty keeping up with her.

'Did you enjoy the concert?' he asked as they circuited the camellia garden.

'Thank you. Yes.'

'Franco and Sofia are good company, too.'

'Vin,' she spoke firmly, 'I am not in the mood for polite conversation.'

'Mmm . . .' He sounded thoughtful. 'A pity, on such a lovely night. Did you notice the moon?'

'I can't say I did.'

'It was so clear. It was as if someone had painted it in the sky,' Vin continued with his monologue. 'No-one takes the time to look up. There's a whole world out there but we are so wrapped up in our own lives we don't realise it.'

'Right now I am more than wrapped up in mine.' May gritted her teeth so tightly her jaw ached.

'That's the reason we need to talk.' Vin held the studio door open for her.

'And for your information,' May swept through, 'I did notice the stars.'

'Was that why Franco passed you his handkerchief during the performance? Did the stars get to you?'

Unable to think of a suitable retort, May shrugged off her wrap. The shutters had been closed, the curtains pulled and the lights dimmed, creating a velvet soft romantic atmosphere. Gentle music played in the background. May had never felt less romantic in her life.

She glanced across to the coffee table. A bottle of wine had been uncorked and placed in an ice bucket alongside two glasses.

'I suggest the first thing we do is sit down, pour ourselves a glass and drink some wine.'

May kicked off her sandals and massaged her feet. She didn't trust herself to speak and the rhythmic movement of her fingers helped to calm her jangled nerves.

'Your poor feet,' Vin sympathised after putting a call through to the kitchen for supper to be delivered to the studio. 'Go easy on them. None of what has happened is their fault.'

'But it is yours,' May hissed at him.

Vin raised his eyebrows at her.

'Perhaps you'd tell me what I've done?'

'It's what you haven't done.'

'What is bugging you now?'

'Why didn't you tell me about your father?'

'My father?' Vin repeated slowly.

'Was it his idea to ask you to get me to stay on, to play the lover?'

A cautious look crossed Vin's face.

'My father runs a garage. He doesn't even know you.'

'Correct me if I'm wrong but didn't he used to be a policeman?' Before Vin could respond May continued. 'In charge of bringing my mother to justice?'

'A moment, please . . . ' Vin cautioned.

'Here, you'd better take these.' May removed her earrings.

'May, listen to me.'

'They're part of the missing haul, aren't they?'

When Vin wouldn't accept the earrings she placed them on the coffee table.

'No wonder you knew what they were worth. It makes sense now.'

'May, please,' Vin implored, 'give me a chance to put my side of the story.'

'You want stories? You can go to your father and tell him you have found the daughter of his jewel thief for him. Is that good enough for you?' May snatched up her glass and swallowed some wine.

'And you can wipe that triumphant smirk off your face.' She spilt some wine as she banged her glass back down on the table.

'You know you're really not very good at being sophisticated, are you? Your hair has fallen out of its ridiculous bun thing.' Vin paused. 'Actually dishevelled makes you look more human, less of an ice queen.'

May put a hand to her collapsed hairdo in an attempt to tuck stray strands back in place.

'I should give up,' Vin advised and held up a small dish of walnuts. 'Here, have one of these, they might calm you down.'

'I do not need calming down.'

Vin placed the dish back on the table.

'As you've had your say, I'll now have mine. My father has no interest in jewel thieves and neither have I. I admit was concerned for Sr Lombardi's safety when I saw you hanging around outside the villa gates the day we met. I wanted to know what you were doing.

'Later, when I saw your earrings I was intrigued as to how they came into your possession. That is all. You do believe me, don't you?'

'Give me one good reason.'

'I don't tell lies.'

'Neither do I and my mother is not a jewel thief.'

'That's why you have to stay on. To prove your mother's innocence and to find out what happened all those years ago.'

May suspected she had backed herself into a corner.

'It's all been such of a shock,' she admitted. 'I am so close to my mother yet she never gave the slightest hint of any of this.'

'I sympathise. Anyone would feel the same in your situation.'

'Tish is one of the most honest people I know.'

'Let's look at this logically. What do you think happened?'

'She must have run away before she could clear her name. Sofia Napoli said the culprits were never caught.'

'That's my take on the situation, too.'

'What about your father? Doesn't he know what happened?'

'If he did he wouldn't say. He never talked about his work and this case happened over twenty-five years ago.'

'Surely there are records?'

'You could try the local newspaper office. There were full reports made out at the time.'

'I'm convinced Florence knows more

than she is saying. And Lis Gilbert, the missing member of the group, what happened to her? She has completely disappeared. Why? And why would my mother never tell me anything about anything?'

Vin poured out more wine.

'You need a change of scenery,' he insisted. 'The autodromo will be closed tomorrow. Auguste holds an annual garden party for the staff. This year it coincides with his birthday celebrations.'

'I'm not a member of staff.'

'Which is why you need not attend — I will take you for a drive along the coast and show you some of the local beauty spots.'

'Surely Auguste would expect you to be present at the party.'

'I'll ask Florence to represent me.' There was a tap at the door. 'Here's our supper.' Vin took delivery of the tray. 'It looks like the chef has prepared a Quattro Stagioni for us.'

'What's that?'

'A Four Seasons pizza. Do you like

Mozzarella or how about tomato and olives?'

Exhausted by the day's events, May was forced to stifle a yawn behind the back of her hand.

'And,' Vin added, segmenting the pizza, 'I promise not to outstay my welcome.'

He was as good as his word and left as soon as they finished their supper.

'We both need an early night. I'll see myself out.'

As May was preparing for bed she heard a text ping into her inbox. Suspecting it may be from her mother asking why she had not been in touch she decided not to respond.

No Further Forward

May awoke late the next morning, refreshed and feeling more like her usual self. A maid had already tidied the studio, pulled back the curtains and cleared away the remnants of last night's pizza supper. After her shower May decided to spend the morning checking up on the local newspaper reports filed at the time of the jewel robberies.

'Si, signorina,' the maid replied to her request, 'a car and driver will be outside for you in ten minutes.'

After dressing in casual top and trousers, May grabbed her bag and notebook headed outside. A young driver was waiting by the main gates.

'You wish to go to the records office?' he asked as he held open the door of a scarlet low-slung roadster, the hubs of its sports wheels gleaming in the morning sun.

'Thank you.'

May settled into the passenger seat. With the top down she had a chance to take in the local scenery. Since her arrival she had not been able to explore the area. The villa was sheltered on one side by a backdrop of surrounding hills and in the distance she could hear a woodpecker in action. She leaned back in her seat and let the sun's rays warm her face.

Was this where her roots lay? Was her father Italian?

A crocodile of children waved as they drove by and an old man struggling up the hill with a heavily laden donkey paused to let them pass on the narrow road leading down to Bella Acqua.

As they descended the hill, the white sails of the yachts created a stunning contrast to the deep turquoise water of the lake. A woman emerging on to a first floor villa balcony threw some bed linen over the rails allowing it to air. She greeted May as her driver slowed up for the crossroads.

'You go up in the world. No more smelly taxis for you.' Betta cast an appreciative glance at the car's paintwork.

May smiled and waved back.

'All is well with you?' Betta called out.

The car drove off before May could reply. She gave a backwards wave but did not turn round so missed the thoughtful expression in Betta's eyes.

A few minutes later the driver pulled up outside a dark grey building that looked more like a monastery than a records office.

An imposing Roman statue dominated the square overshadowing the building.

'Is this the right place?' May asked.

'Si. It was once inhabited by Bene-dictine monks, signorina, but for many years now it has housed all local records. What time would you like me to collect you?'

'One hour?' May did not hold out much hope that her search would be successful but she knew she had to try.

He responded with a noisy rev of his engine and drove off, pretending not to notice the admiring glances of a trio of young girls gathered by the traffic lights.

May mounted the steps leading to the records office. Inside she met a warren of corridors and signs indicating various libraries and archive stores.

She stopped a passing official.

'Newspaper records?' she asked in hesitant English.

'What century?'

'Er, twenty-five years ago?'

'Follow me, please.'

The office was hidden away at the back of the building and looked as though it had at one time been a kitchen. Hooks still hung from the ceiling and a huge fireplace had been converted into a small reading area.

A smiling official took down May's details then returned with a list of numbers indicating the area where she would find the relevant newspaper editions she was looking for. She took them to a desk in the corner. May struggled with her translation of the reports but it wasn't difficult to gather the jewel thieves had targeted mainly high-profile residents of the area.

At the top of one report there was a photograph of two women. With a sick feeling in the pit of her stomach May recognised her mother and although the second photograph was blurred the caption identified her as Lis Gilbert, the other half of the Beautiful Twins. May had to agree Lis possessed a stunning Nordic beauty.

There were passing references to Vin's father Alberto and pictures of his team carrying out their investigations.

The assistant approached May.

'There is a young man outside asking for you.'

Startled to realise she had spent more than an hour perusing the records May stood up and thanked the assistant for her help.

'You have been reading up about our famous jewel robberies?' the assistant enquired, glancing at the newspaper articles.

'Do you remember them?' May asked.

'I was fifteen at the time but I recall there was a beautiful blonde lady suspected of being involved. Are you writing a book?'

'My mother was the other lady in the picture.' May indicated the photograph. 'Do you remember her?'

The assistant shook her head.

'I believe one of the ladies ran away to get married but it may only have been gossip. It was a long time ago. I am sorry I cannot be of more help.'

* * *

'There you are,' Florence greeted her after she returned to the studio at Villa Lombardi. 'Lunch is a buffet on the terrace and I've come to collect you.'

May had forgotten to eat breakfast and her stomach reminded her that she was hungry.

'Will Sr Lombardi be present?' she asked.

'Auguste is resting in preparation for this afternoon's garden party. I understand you and Vin are giving it a miss because he's taking you for a drive?'

116

'He thought I should see some of the local scenery.'

'He has asked me to deputise in his absence.' Florence cast May a speculative look. 'Where have you been all morning?'

'Down at the records office.'

'What were you doing there?'

'I'm trying to find out more about the jewel robberies.'

'And did you discover anything?'

'Not much more than I already knew.'

A group of people was standing around the terrace chatting. To her relief May saw they were mainly autodromo employees, most of whom gave her a friendly smile.

'It's a holiday today.' Florence picked up two plates. 'And with the fine weather we are all making the best of our day off. Tuck in.' She indicated the table groaning with local delicacies.

'Do you know why Lis and Tish split up?' May asked as she and Florence sat down on two of the garden chairs.

Florence bit into a breadstick.

'I can tell you why I split with them. It was Andreas,' she said. 'Before he worked for Auguste, he was a chauffeur for a businessman and I kept bumping into him all over the place.

'When the girls were performing I had time to kill, so Andreas and I would go for a walk. A walk became a drink and a drink became a meal. One day,' Florence paused. 'I do not know what was wrong with Lis; she could be very artistic.

'Looking back, I think she wanted an excuse for a fight with someone and she chose me.

'There were stories she had a high profile boyfriend and the business of the burglaries unsettled her. She said they were bad for her image. I'm afraid she was very self-centred.'

'Was the boyfriend Hector Lombardi?'

'It is possible,' Florence acknowledged.

'Hector wasn't involved with my mother, was he?'

'Hector liked blonde girl friends. He wasn't interested in Tish or me.'

'And your argument with Lis — what

was that about?' May prompted.

'I'm not sure now.' Florence turned her attention away from May as if reluctant to look her in the eye.

'Can't you remember anything?' May asked.

Florence nodded.

'I will tell you what I do remember. After our argument Lis stormed off. Andreas, who couldn't help overhearing what had happened, seized his chance and asked me to marry him. It was totally out of the blue.

'You see, Sr Lombardi had offered him a job. Andreas was unhappy in his current employment. His boss didn't treat him well so he decided to move on. I was so annoyed with Lis I accepted Andreas's proposal. I hate to admit I left the girls in the lurch but I was growing disenchanted with the lifestyle.

'The open road has its challenges and we were always driving to another party and Lis was growing increasingly difficult.'

'Did you tell Tish and Lis you were

119

leaving?'

'I left a note for them. I didn't trust myself to talk to Lis after the way things were left between us.'

'I see.'

'I think that is probably why your mother did not keep in touch with me. I behaved badly.'

'So you moved here?'

'Within a short time Hector had his accident, I Bei Gemelli split up and that part of my life was over.'

'Vin says my earrings are genuine emeralds and diamonds.'

'What can I say?' Florence sounded evasive. 'You could have them valued, I suppose.'

'Vin also says they are part of the Lombardi collection.'

The expression on Florence's face now convinced May she knew far more than she was saying.

'Do you think they were stolen?' May persisted.

'If you are asking me if they were proceeds of a robbery then I am certain they were not.'

'If they are genuine how did they come into my mother's possession?'

'Tish was not a thief, neither was Lis.' Florence looked angry. 'Of course we had our differences. What group of girls doesn't? But of one thing I am sure — they were good girls.

'They were honest and I would have known if either of them had done any-thing underhand. They were usually so tired after their gigs all they wanted to do was relax.

'They had no time to run around steal-ing jewellery. You must not think such a thing. Nobody ever proved anything against any of us for the simple reason we were innocent.'

'Why the raised voices?' Vin strolled towards them.

'You wouldn't understand.' Florence looked close to tears as she stood up and pushed him away.

'I think,' Vin watched a stiff backed Florence stalk off, 'I haven't arrived a moment too soon.'

May put her plate down on the table. 'I have to go after her and apologise.'

'Leave her alone for a while,' Vin advised. 'Florence doesn't sulk. I'm sure she is still your friend. She needs time on her own, that's all. Come on, I'll take you for that drive.'

A Sudden Halt

'How many cars do you have?' May eyed up the highly polished black convertible parked outside the villa.

'I have none. There is a pool of vehicles,' Vin explained. 'They all belong to the Foundation. We have to sign in and sign out every time we use one and give a good business reason for our journey.'

'Was I a good business reason?'

'You are Sr Lombardi's guest and that is reason enough. The pool system works well and is rarely abused. There are certain cars the young mechanics are not allowed to drive.'

'Because they like to show off?' May thought of her morning driver.

'Young men are young men and Foundation jobs are much sought after. Applicants are subjected to rigorous tests so being seen driving a fast car is like a badge of office.'

'Were you subjected to these rigorous

123

tests?'

Vin cast May a sideways glance as they drove off in the direction of the lake.

'I always loved things mechanical. I went to engineering college and soon realised cars were my first love. I decided I didn't want to do anything else but work with cars so I wrote to many influential men.

'When Auguste replied I read up on all the work he had done improving road safety and setting up a scholarship for young drivers who might not be able to afford the training. I knew I had to work for him so in answer to your question, yes, I did the tests.'

'How long ago was this?'

'I was twenty-three when I started work at the autodromo. I'm now thirty,' he smiled, 'if you were wondering.'

'I'm not, but I am wondering why Sr Lombardi offered you such a responsible job at such a young age.'

'He never really found anyone to replace Andreas. Things had been going downhill at the autodromo. Sr Lombardi had lost heart and was not in the best of health.

'Four years ago he gave me six months to prove I could turn the business round. There was a lot at stake and I worked all day, every day. It was hard work but I loved every moment of it.' He cast May a sideways look.

'I'm still here so I think Sr Lombardi approves of all that I have done.'

The car began a slow descent down to the neighbouring village to Acqua Bella.

'Would you like a coffee?' Vin asked. 'An espresso, perhaps? I know the place to go and you didn't get much lunch, did you?'

Vin parked in a shady corner of the main square.

'You'd better hang on to me,' he held out his hand, 'otherwise we might get separated.'

'I can manage,' May insisted.

'I don't doubt it but one of the less attractive aspects of tourist resorts in this area is pick-pocketing. You'll be quite safe if you stick with me but if you want to go it alone hang on to your purse.'

'I have nothing worth taking.' May put a hand around her shoulder bag.

'You have credit cards, a passport, money, a mobile phone, don't you?'

'Yes,' May conceded. 'Is it far to the coffee shop?' she asked.

'A ten-minute walk and I am getting hot standing in the sun wasting time on a pointless discussion. Are we in this together?'

May deciding further resistance was futile, nodded. Vin's hand was firm and warm against hers and she was glad she had chosen not to reject his offer. Acqua Maggiore was a bustling community, full of tourists and day visitors who Vin informed her had come to view the famous marble sculptures in the chapel on the hill.

On more than one occasion, groups coming from the opposite direction jostled against them. It would be easy for someone to dip a hand into a bag or pocket.

They arrived at an artisan café tucked

away down a side street leading on to a small square. Tables had been set up outside under a striped awning and the proprietor seemed to know all his customers as he moved from table to table refilling glasses and exchanging gossip.

'Vincenzo!' He extended his arms then, ignoring Vin, embraced an unsuspecting May in a bear hug.

He beamed at her, releasing her from his hold and looking hard at her.

'You are English, I think, but I detect Italian blood. I can see you have the Roman fire in your veins. Now, please, sit down. I will bring you the speciality of the house.' He kissed May on both cheeks.

'Who was that?' May's eyes were wide with surprise as she tried to recover her composure.

'Tonio. He and his wife have been running their café for many years.'

A young waitress returned with a tray of coffee and pastries oozing apples and almonds and candied peel. May wiped the last vestige of icing sugar from her lips as she leaned back against her seat with a satisfied sigh. The afternoon sun had changed angle and she could feel it beating on the back of her neck.

'If you've finished, I suggest we walk off some of our indulgence.'

Vin stood up and with Tonio's blessing ringing in their ears as he eyed up their empty plates, Vin led May back down the way they had come.

'There will be fewer people around now,' he explained. 'It is the hottest part of the day and the locals like to rest for an hour or two. They keep late hours so an afternoon siesta is a good idea.'

'What are we going to do?'

'Continue our drive around the lake?' Vin suggested.

'Is that the famous chapel?' May pointed up to the hill to where a white building dominated the skyline.

'It is indeed. You know it has a secret passageway down to the lake? It was built apparently so the monks could escape in case of attack.'

'From whom?'

'I'm not too sure but someone was always fighting someone else back then, so take your pick.'

'It seems so peaceful here that it's hard to imagine a war.'

'We'd better get on,' Vin urged. 'I want to show you some of the villas your mother would have visited.'

It wasn't difficult to identify the properties belonging to the rich and famous, although most of them were shielded from the road by high walls or trees.

'Some are holiday homes and unoccupied a lot of the time,' Vin explained as they drove past another set of padlocked gates, 'but in the high season there is entertainment of some sort almost every night.'

'And my mother and her friend Lis would have performed at these parties?'

'I would think so. Florence could probably tell you more about it.'

'Vin.' May turned to him. 'You don't think I am over-reacting, do you? I mean, all this talk about robberies and stolen jewels — it's like something out of a film and I can't believe it's happening to me.'

'It does seem incredible,' he acknowledged, 'especially after what I said about your earrings. Where are they, by the way?'

'I didn't want them going missing so as a precaution I've locked them away in the safe in my room.'

'You can't be too careful,' Vin approved. 'Your arrival has stirred things up and I'm sure I'm not the only one who noticed them at the party.'

'Do you think someone would try to steal them?'

'I don't know what to think,' Vin admitted, 'but from what you've told me I believe your mother was innocent and not involved in all the robberies that were going on.'

'It still doesn't explain why she would never tell me about my father or why I was born in Milan.'

'Agreed — but not telling you about her past does not make her a criminal.'

May was jolted forward in her seat as the engine stuttered and misfired before the car shuddered to a halt.

'What's happened?'

'I'm not sure.' Vin leaped out of the driver's seat and raised the bonnet.

'Can you see anything?'

'You're not going to believe this . . . .' He stopped, a frown creasing his forehead.

'What?' They were a long way from anywhere and she hadn't realised quite how remote it was up in the hills. The idea of being stranded here sent an uneasy shiver up her spine.

'We've run out of petrol.'

Bizarre Situation

You're not serious.' May stared at Vin in disbelief.

'These things happen.' Vin's voice echoed May's disbelief. 'I should have checked the gauge before we set off but I was running late.'

'You don't expect me to fall for such an old trick?'

'I didn't do it on purpose,' Vin replied through gritted teeth. 'The mechanics frequently use the cars. Any one of them could have forgotten to refill the tank.'

'Don't blame the mechanics.'

'Wait here.' Vin yanked open his door.

'Where are you going?' May demanded.

'To get petrol.'

'I'm coming with you.'

'As you wish.'

They trudged down the hill in taut silence.

'There's a garage.' May pointed to a run-down building at the side of the road. She peered at a notice dangling off a padlock. 'Does chiuso mean what I think it means?'

'It means closed,' Vin responded in a tight voice.

'Hadn't you better telephone one of your mechanics and ask them to come and rescue us or are you too ashamed to admit you got it wrong?' May grinned.

'Auguste has given everyone a day's holiday. They will all be at the garden party.'

'Surely someone is on duty.'

'There will be a guard at the gate but he can't leave his post.'

'Can't you get him to pass on a message saying we are stranded and that it's an emergency?' May was losing patience with Vin. It sounded as though he was making excuses for not calling for help.

'May I borrow your mobile?'

'Where's yours?'

'I don't know,' Vin admitted. 'I might have left it in the office. I told you I left in a hurry.'

'And my bag is in the car,' May replied.

'How long would it take us to walk back?'

'Half an hour?' Vin hazarded a guess.

Still fuming, May marched over to the garage and banged loudly on the door. There was no response. An advert attached to a grubby window caught her attention.

'Pensione,' she read out loud. 'Do you think La Villa Della Pesca is far from here?'

Vin stood beside May and read the details of the holiday accommodation.

'It will probably be closed up.'

'Surely it's worth a try,' May insisted, 'and we know they have a landline.' She pointed to the contact number.

Vin nodded agreement.

'Let's give it a go,' he said.

'We are not open,' an unfriendly voice informed them over the speaker attached to the entry gates.

A rapid conversation followed as Vin explained their predicament. Unable to catch all they were saying, May moved away and bumped into an elderly lady standing behind her.

'Problem?' she asked.

'With our car,' May agreed.

'And you need help?'

'The garage is closed and we saw an advert for accommodation.' May's voice trailed away as she was subjected to an intense inspection.

'This is where I live,' the elderly lady explained. With a regal gesture she nudged Vin out of the way. 'Open the gates at once, Alba,' she ordered, 'and admit our guests.'

'Thank you, signora,' May said.

'You may address me as Contessa.'

'I'm sorry — Contessa,' May corrected.

'At once,' she repeated her command to the unfortunate Alba who was still issuing a vigorous protest.

'We wouldn't want to put you to any bother.' Vin stepped forward.

'And you are?'

'Vincenzo Piace.'

'I am the Contessa Novelli,' she announced. 'And this,' she waved one of her spaniel's paws at them, 'is Drago.

We have been for a walk and now we are tired.'

'We're not looking for a room,' Vin insisted. 'If we could make one telephone call?'

'We'd be prepared to pay,' May added, 'or if we give you the number, you could make the call for us.'

The Contessa's scathing look suggested such an idea was preposterous.

'We don't open to guests until next month,' she explained.

'We understand,' Vin said.

'But in this case I am prepared to make an exception,' the Contessa responded, the tone of her voice suggesting that her word was law. 'We will have an enjoyable supper together after which you can test our facilities for our paying guests, then in the morning you may make your telephone call. Where have you come from?'

'Bella Acqua,' Vin replied.

'But you are English, I think?' She turned to May. 'What is your name?'

'May Maxwell.'

'And you are from Bella Acqua also?'

'I am staying there.'

'Do you know Auguste Lombardi?'

'Vin is his chief mechanic and we've run out of petrol,' May replied. 'That's why we need to use your telephone.'

The Contessa burst into a peal of laughter.

'The old excuses are the best, aren't they? Has that one come back into fashion?'

'It wasn't deliberate,' a red-faced Vin protested.

'No matter, you are here now and you must call me Rosamunde,' the Contessa insisted.

They began walking down the path leading to the villa.

'I was sorry not to make Auguste's party.' She sighed. 'But these days I find social occasions tiring. Please give him my regards when next you see him.'

'You know Sr Lombardi?' Vin enquired.

'He's an old friend.'

By now they had reached the villa. The austere brickwork of its peach-coloured stone was softened by the angle of the sun. A stern-faced woman stood on the steps blocking the main entrance.

'There's no need for concern,' Rosamunde confided to May with a twinkle in her eye. 'Alba goes home at sunset.'

'Contessa,' Alba chided, her face softening, 'I have excellent hearing.'

'Good,' Rosamunde responded, 'in that case perhaps you would get our guests some refreshments. What is on the menu for dinner tonight?'

'Proscuitto and salad, grilled trout followed by apricots and almonds baked in honey.'

'Perfect. Please bring up a bottle of white wine from the cellar and while we are waiting we'll have some English tea. Would you like to go through to the terrace while I freshen up and see to Drago?'

'Who are these people?' she heard Alba interrogating Rosamunde as they disappeared inside.

'Old friends,' Rosamunde replied. 'Now don't make a fuss.'

May settled down in one of the cane

chairs overlooking the bay far below.

'What do we do now?' she asked Vin who sat down beside her.

'You have an expression in your country — go with the flow.'

'Can we trust our hostess? I mean she says she's a friend of Auguste's, but we've no way of checking and she won't let us use her telephone. That's hardly normal behaviour, is it?'

'I have heard of the slightly eccentric Contessa Novelli but I had no idea this was where she lived.'

'Can't you get us out of this ridiculous situation?'

'What do you suggest I do?'

'I don't know but you got us into it.' May couldn't stop herself from sounding grouchy.

'We can't use the Contessa's telephone without her permission. You say your mobile's in the car?'

'Yes.'

'In that case . . . ' Vin leaped to his feet.

'Where are you going?' May demanded.

'To fetch your mobile but I need to go now before it gets dark.'

Before May could stop him, Vin had exited through the open French windows and disappeared around the side of the villa.

May took a few moments out to catch her breath and think things through. Had she been the victim of a sophisticated kidnap plan? She jumped to her feet. If she were quick she might be able to catch up with Vin.

'Where are you going, signorina?' Alba appeared carrying a tray of tea things.

'My companion, Sr Piace . . .' she began.

'Has left,' Alba replied, 'on the Contessa's motor scooter.'

May's legs refused to support her and she sank back into her cane chair.

'He's left?'

'Do not worry,' Alba added with the ghost of a smile, 'the Contessa is not riding pillion. She rarely uses her scooter now but it still has a small amount of fuel in the tank and it should be enough for Sr Piace to run his errand.'

'English tea, how lovely,' Rosamunde trilled from the doorway.

'I have laid out everything you need for your supper, Contessa,' Alba explained.

'Thank you. We can look after ourselves if you want to go home.' Rosamunde leaned forward and picked up a sweet biscuit. 'Alba saves these for special occasions. She must like you.'

'She doesn't know anything about me.' May followed Rosamunde's example. Her pastry snack now seemed a long time ago.

'But I do.' Rosamunde leaned back in her seat and bit into her biscuit. 'You're Tish Delacourt's daughter.'

Another Piece of
the Puzzle

'I spotted the resemblance immediately but I wasn't sure until you said you were English. Then I knew.'

'You knew my mother?' May's heart was pounded so loudly she could hardly hear her own voice.

'She was one of The Twins, wasn't she?' Rosamunde's eyes sparkled with delight at the memory. 'You've got the same colour of eyes. They were so unusual it drove the young men wild. I was madly jealous.'

'Where did you meet her?'

'Have some tea,' Rosamunde urged, 'and you must try one of those coconut bites.'

To please her, May poured out two cups of tea in the delicate cups provided and took one of the small biscuits.

'Where did I meet Tish?' Rosamunde pondered the question. 'I can't remember exactly. I suppose it must have been at a party. In those days Migoleto and I were invited everywhere.

'Your mother and her friend would entertain us and afterwards there would be a buffet or reception or some such. We held many parties here. The girls were such fun.

They would get everyone dancing and tapping their toes. The music was so vibrant.

'They were always late arriving but that added to their charisma. People didn't mind waiting. Their transport would break down but with an army of young men on hand to help out no-one seemed to care. They could write their own rules. Things were done differently in those days.'

'Do you know anything about the jewel robberies?' May seized her chance to interrogate the Contessa before Vin returned.

'A sad business. I lost some rings. Stupidly I left them in the bathroom and when I went back for them they had disappeared. I asked around but no-one had seen them. They were never recovered.'

'My mother was a suspect, wasn't she?'

'We all were. The same crowd went to the same parties. The police interviewed everyone.'

'Do you think my mother was involved?'

'Heavens, no, she and her friends were out to have fun. They weren't criminals. Is your mother here with you?' Rosamunde leaned forward, an eager look on her face. 'I would like to see her again.'

'She doesn't know I am here.'

'I sense intrigue. If it's not too impertinent a question, what are you doing here?'

'Do you know Florence Amaria?'

'Not well, but we have met on occasions. She left the group, as I recall.'

'She was their driver. Her husband Andreas was also a chauffeur.'

'I remember now. He worked for a man none of us liked.' The Contessa wrinkled her nose. 'A bulky individual with horrid eyes and bulbous lips. You had the feeling he was working out how much you were worth. What happened to Andreas?'

'He got a job working for Sr Lombardi and after he died Florence stayed on.'

'It was Florence who sent out the invitations for Auguste's birthday party, wasn't it?'

'Yes.'

'Did your mother also receive one?'

'Yes.'

'Which you acquired?' Rosamunde raised a plucked eyebrow.

'It fell into my hands.'

'And you came out here without her knowledge?' Rosamunde waited expectantly for May's answer.

'Yes.'

'May I ask why?'

'I was born in Milan,' May explained, 'but my mother would never talk about her time in Italy. All I want to know is why.'

'And you bumped into all sorts of nonsense about her being a jewel thief.'

'She gave me a pair of earrings for my twenty-third birthday. Everyone is saying they are real diamonds and emeralds. I thought they were costume. I don't know what to make of anything.'

'Please don't think I am speaking out of turn . . . ' Rosamunde paused as if uncertain how to continue.

'Anything you can tell me would be of help,' May urged. 'All the people I have spoken to have a connection with Auguste and I'm not sure who to believe.'

'It was a long time ago and my memory is not what it used to be,' Rosamunde admitted.

May bit down her disappointment.

'You see there was so much happening at the time and I have to admit in those days I was rather selfish. We were all very self-centred. I shudder with shame when I remember the way we behaved.

'We didn't notice what was going on around us. We were wrapped up in our little world but I can't help feeling some of the people who lost their jewels deserved to be robbed and I include myself. It's not a nice thing to say but I am afraid it is true.'

'No-one seems to remember much about what happened,' May admitted.

'Florence was on the scene at the time and she was at the centre of things,' Rosamunde pointed out.

'She says she's told me all she does know.'

A loud explosion outside made them both jump and caused Drago to bark and run round in excited circles.

'That sounds like my scooter announcing its comeback. Perhaps you'd better check your handsome companion hasn't come to grief.'

Vin was standing beside an ancient motor scooter. He unhooked May's bag off the handlebars. The scooter lurched sideways as it lost its balance.

'This thing's lethal.' Vin tried to straighten it. 'It nearly had me over more than once.' He lodged it under an awning and covered it with a tarpaulin. 'I secured the car and I checked on the garage. It won't be open until nine o'clock tomorrow morning so if Rosa-munde meant what she said, we are going to have to stay overnight.'

'Not if I have anything to do with it.' May waved her mobile in the air. 'I can't get a signal. This is too ridiculous for words. We have to get back tonight.'

'Do we?'

'Of course we do. How can you even ask such a thing?'

'You need time away from the villa and the Contessa is a nice lady. It wouldn't do any harm to stay over.'

Drago came running towards them, nipping at their ankles. Vin scooped him up.

'Now we are here,' he said, 'we may as well enjoy ourselves. Wouldn't you say, Drago?'

The dog nuzzled his ear.

'I'm still not entirely sure what's going on,' May protested. 'It's almost as if you arranged to break down.'

'You didn't think I deserted you on purpose, did you?'

May flushed, uncertain how to

respond.

'It crossed my mind,' she admitted. 'I mean, Alba and Rosamunde disappeared, you rode off on a moped. I've got no idea where I am.'

'And you thought you were being held hostage?' Vin's face lit up with amusement. 'I'd love to know why. Did you think I was after your emeralds? I mean, with you locked up here I could have raced back to the villa and stolen them.'

'Now you're being ridiculous.'

'And you're not thinking straight. An overnight stay in this beautiful villa is exactly what you need — a complete change of scenery.'

'Come along,' Rosamunde commanded from the terrace, 'your tea is getting cold.'

'I meant what I said,' Vin repeated. 'We work together. Agreed?'

'Agreed,' May nodded.

'And no more talk about kidnap plots.'

May realised it would be counterproductive not to trust Vin.

'I do have something to tell you,'

she said.

'Yes?'

'Rosamunde knew my mother.'

'Now that is a lead.'

'I don't like being kept waiting,' the Contessa's voice rang out again.

'We'd best do as our hostess says.' Vin urged May towards the terrace, 'Let's hope she lets slip something else of importance.'

The evening shadows lengthened as, over supper, Rosamunde revealed details of her past life when she and Migoleto travelled the world.

'He was a scoundrel,' she said, 'but I loved him and in his way he loved me, but he left me far too soon and with dreadful debts.'

'So you opened up the villa to visitors?' May asked.

'I had to do something after he died. Luckily the villa was in my name and this area is very popular with tourists. I guarantee complete discretion, so,' she added with the familiar naughty twinkle in her eye, 'I am always in demand. Any secrets you have are safe with me.'

'We are not hiding any secrets,' Vin said with a stern note in his voice.

'May has a secret in her past.'

'One I know nothing about,' May insisted.

'But you are learning and that is why you are here, is it not?'

'We had no idea of your connection to my mother.'

'I thought that was the reason you wanted to stay over.'

'That was your suggestion,' Vin broke in.

'Maybe it was.' Rosamunde sounded supremely unconcerned by his allegation.

'It was,' May affirmed. 'Why did you want us to stay over?'

Rosamunde shifted uncomfortably.

'If you must know I get lonely. I don't get out too often these days.' A sad look crossed her face. 'Darlings, it has been absolutely wonderful having your company over dinner but if you really want to leave, I suppose I can't stop you.'

May and Vin exchanged an awkward glance.

'We'll stay.' It was Vin who made the decision.

Rosamunde clapped her hands in delight.

'Wonderful. Please avail yourself of all the facilities. I need my beauty sleep so I will retire to my room. Enjoy the rest of your evening together and finish the wine. It's from a local vineyard and I'd like to know what you think of it.

'If it meets with your approval I will offer it to my summer guests. You will find everything you need on the first floor. Choose whichever rooms you like. They are all en suite and fully furnished.'

'She's quite an act, isn't she?' Vin said after Rosamunde and Drago had departed.

'She told me she and her husband were friends of Auguste. They moved in the same circles, the party set, and my mother and Lis used to entertain them.'

'Did they indeed? It's another lead, isn't it?'

152

'I asked Rosamunde about the jewel robberies and she said everyone was a suspect.'

'I don't think we are going to get any more out of her now she's retired for the night.' Vin held up the wine bottle. 'We'd better finish this if we're going to do a report.'

The bubbles sparkled in the reflection of the candles Rosamunde had lit and placed on the table.

'Do you regret your decision to come out to Bella Acqua?' Vin's question took May by surprise.

She toyed thoughtfully with the stem of her wine glass.

'Whatever secret my mother was hiding it concerns me and it is time I knew about it. I don't know if she was ever going to tell me what happened, so no I don't regret it, whatever the consequences.'

'Good — because I don't regret meeting you, despite your suspicions about me being an agent of my father.'

Vin edged his chair to May's. Gentle

raindrops fell, washing the leaves of Rosamunde's red and pink potted geraniums a deep green.

'Please . . . ' Not sure of his intentions May backed away from Vin. 'I don't need any more complications in my life.'

'You've gone through a lot of emotion recently, haven't you? Why don't you take Rosamunde's advice and enjoy what the evening has to offer? Her guests pay to stay here. We're getting the full treatment free.'

As an actor, May had heard many such lines delivered both on and off the stage and she could spot a phoney a mile off. Up until now she had thought Vin was genuine. She twirled her glass between her fingers.

'I know that.'

'But?' Vin prompted.

'Running out of petrol? Even Rosamunde saw through that one.'

Vin frowned.

'You're right.'

'You mean you arranged to break down on purpose?'

'I can't help feeling the tank has been tampered with.'

May shook her head in bewilderment.

'Who would do such a thing and why?'

'I wish I knew.' Vin stood up, 'but as I'm fresh out of ideas I'll see if I can find an umbrella.'

'What?'

'We are going to take a stroll through the gardens before we turn in for the night. You'd best blow out the candles. We don't want to set the place on fire.'

Vin and May stood on the balustrade overlooking the pinprick lights of Acqua Maggiore studding the hazy night air. Gentle drops of rain pattered on their golfing umbrella. Music drifted up from the valley below.

'It's strange to think perhaps my mother stood on this very spot.'

Vin's fingers touched May's.

'Maybe you should let the past go.'

'It's all very well for you to say that but you know who your parents are.'

'I'm sure your mother had her reasons for not telling you about your father.'

155

'I have a right to know.' May pounded the balustrade with her bunched fist. 'It's not too much to ask, is it?'

Vin placed his arm around her shoulders.

'You're shivering,' he said, his body warm beside hers, 'and the rain's turning heavy. We'd better go inside.'

May mounted the creaky wooden stairs to the first floor while Vin locked up.

'I don't suppose it matters which room we take,' he paused as he followed her on to the landing and opened the nearest door. 'Sleep well.' He kissed her on both cheeks.

May chose the room next to Vin's and as she closed the door her bag vibrated against her shoulder. The mobile signal had come too late for her to arrange transport back to the villa. With a sigh of irritation she inspected her texts and, with a sense of growing dismay, she read the one from her mother.

Startling News

One of the maids tapped on May's bed-room door.

'Sr Lombardi would like you to join him for coffee, signorina.'

The direct drive back to Bella Acqua that morning had taken less than half an hour and May was still gathering her scattered thoughts as she tried to think through the events of the past 24 hours.

Alba informed her and Vin over a light croissant breakfast that the Contessa liked to sleep late and would not wish to be disturbed. She promised to make their goodbyes for them.

To May's surprise Alba had also arranged for a can of petrol to be delivered from the local garage to the villa.

Vin had seemed as eager as May to be on his way. May still could not shake off the suspicion that the car had not run out of fuel by accident and that Vin was somehow behind what had happened.

Had he wanted her kept out of Auguste's way?

They had spoken little on the journey home, May preoccupied with her mother's late-night text and Vin concentrating on the road ahead. Drops of rain splashed the windscreen, forcing him to raise the hood of the car reducing the seating space and creating a cramped stuffy atmosphere. May seized the chance to re-read the message from Tish.

Flying back home tomorrow, important meeting at head office. See u soon. Xxx

'Signorina?' the maid prompted May when there was no response.

'Sorry, yes.' May dragged her thoughts back to the present. 'I'm coming.'

Sheltering under an umbrella emblazoned with the family crest, May and the maid crossed the camellia garden and entered the main house to where Auguste was waiting for May in the drawing-room.

'Good morning. Pour out some coffee, if you would be so kind,' Auguste said in a tone of voice she had not heard before.

With a growing sense of unease, May did as she was told.

'Then perhaps you can tell me why you did not attend my garden party yesterday afternoon or have the courtesy to send an apology for your absence.'

May flushed with embarrassment. She should have realised Auguste was of a generation that set store by such things.

'I am sorry,' she apologised. 'It won't happen again,' she added.

'And can you also supply me with an explanation as to why you did not come home last night?'

May squirmed in her seat. This wrongdoing was going to be more difficult to explain.

'I . . . ' She sipped some coffee to ease the dryness in her throat. 'We ran out of petrol,' she admitted.

'We?' Auguste queried.

'Vin Piace took me for a drive around the lake to show me some of the local sights.'

'And why did you find it necessary to

stay out all night?'

'The local garage was closed and we couldn't get a mobile signal to call for help. We were stranded.'

May knew her explanation sounded weak and she wouldn't blame Auguste if he didn't believe her.

'So where did you spend the night?'

Something in his demeanour convinced May there was more at stake here than idle curiosity.

'At the Villa Della Pesca — it is run by an old friend of yours, the Contessa Rosamunde Novelli. She sent you her best wishes and told us she was sorry she was unable to attend your party.'

'Rosamunde?' The expression on Auguste's face thawed a little. 'How is she?'

'In good health. She opens up her villa in the summer months and she offered us accommodation for the night as she has plenty of rooms. We would have telephoned from her villa but Rosamunde asked us to stay over.'

'And you accepted her invitation?'

'Yes.'

'I am pleased to have news of Rosamunde but disappointed the incident happened. I would have expected better behaviour from Vin.'

'It wasn't his fault,' May insisted.

'Nonetheless, the name of Lombardi has been compromised.'

'In what way?'

'If it hadn't been for Rebecca, I might not have been aware of the situation.'

'She told you what happened?' May stiffened. 'How did she know?'

'Florence called on you last evening. She wanted to apologise for walking out on you over lunch and to tell you about the garden party. She found the studio unoccupied. Rebecca was with her. Apart from anything else I was concerned you might have met with an accident.'

'I really am very sorry. It won't happen again,' she repeated.

'I accept your apology.'

Auguste still sounded as though the matter was not settled.

'But I don't see how I could have

compromised the Lombardi name,' May insisted.

'Don't you?'

'You are treating me like . . . ' May stopped speaking as the full impact of her suspicions took root. 'A member of the family.'

Auguste did not reply.

'Is that what I am?' May plucked up the courage to ask.

Their coffee cooled on the table in front of them. After an agonising wait Auguste shook his head.

'I don't know.'

'I have no wish to distress you,' May said, concerned her enquiries might prove too much for his delicate state of health.

Auguste held up a hand to silence her.

'I have to tell you something which until now has been a closely guarded secret but before I do I need your solemn promise you will not divulge the information to anyone else.'

'I am not sure I could keep such a promise.'

Auguste gave no indication that he had heard her reply.

With a deep sadness etched on his face he was looking across the lake. It reflected his mood, grey and sombre.

'I was out of the country at the time of Hector's accident,' Auguste spoke in an expressionless voice, 'and I did not learn the full details of what happened until it was all over.

'My son wasn't running away with a stash of jewels, neither was he racing his car, nor did he have a pregnant female passenger with him. I have heard all the stories and none of them are true. None of them are even near the truth.'

'You don't have to go on.' May put a hand on Auguste's sleeve, the pain in her chest reminding her to breathe.

'He was actually the victim of a violent kidnapping.'

May gave a gasp as Auguste continued with his story.

'The villains knew I would pay a high ransom for my son's release. What they did not bargain on was Andreas's

163

loyalty.'

'How was Florence's husband involved?'

'In my absence, Andreas had become a role model to my son, a part I should have played had I not been selfishly wrapped up in my own grief. It is something I shall always regret.'

Auguste bowed his head. May was not sure if he would welcome physical contact but she squeezed his fingers.

Auguste held on to May's hand.

'When Andreas realised what had happened,' he went on, 'he raced after the getaway car in an attempt to rescue my son. Andreas was an excellent driver. The kidnapper was not. In the ensuing chase the cars crashed.

'The rest you know. Everyone has at least one version of the story. What the locals don't know they invent, but I have always remained silent on the matter. The affair was hushed up, not because I exerted any influence on the authorities but because they did not want news of the kidnap going public. Events did not reflect well on anyone and I knew nothing would bring my son back.'

'Does Florence know what happened?'

'Like everyone else she thinks what happened was a horrible accident. Her husband was injured but he survived. I chose not to tell Florence all the details and when Andreas recovered some semblance of health he agreed with me.'

'Why have you chosen to tell me your story now?' May asked.

'If you are . . .' he paused ' . . . my granddaughter, I would like to meet up with your mother. She alone knows the truth.' Auguste passed a hand over his forehead. 'Do you think your mother would consider a visit here? I would do my best to make her welcome.'

'From what I have learned she and her friend Lis were more or less accused of being jewel thieves.'

'I did not accuse them of anything. Your mother and her friend attracted much male attention from a group of young men who used them as natural cover for their activities.

'They gained easy access into exclusive

venues by helping load and set up equipment, seeing to the car, making sure everything was working. Their presence raised no suspicion.'

'Are you saying they were the thieves?'

'Many years have passed.' Auguste's voice faded. 'Perhaps I have said too much.'

'Can you tell me anything about my earrings?'

A flash of lightning scarred the sky followed by a distant rumble of thunder. Rain pounded the terrace. A manservant entered the room as hastily as his dignity would allow.

'I said we were not to be interrupted,' Auguste snapped at him.

'I am so sorry, Signore Lombardi, but I have come to tell you there has been an accident at the autodromo.'

Terrible Turn of Events

The circuit of the autodromo was a sea of flashing lights and swarming with high security vested officials as they battled with the heavy rain bouncing off the racetrack.

'What's happened?' May grabbed the arm of a passing mechanic, but his knowledge of English was limited. He gestured with his arms then disappeared into the throng of officials.

There was no sign of Vin or Florence and Auguste had been whisked away by a uniformed official the moment they arrived. May tried to follow them by ducking under the cordon set up around the circuit but another official restrained her.

'No entry,' he said firmly.

The expression on the security guard's face discouraged her from disregarding his orders.

'Rebecca,' she called out as the girl

pushed past her.

A white-faced Rebecca stared blankly back at her. Her shirt was soaked and her hair hung in rats' tails.

'You need to get dry.' May tugged at her arm in an attempt to get a reaction. 'You're shaking with cold.'

'I have to see . . . ' She shook May's hand away.

'No entry,' the guard repeated.

'Inside,' May ordered Rebecca in a firm voice.

The office was deserted and had the appearance of having been abandoned in a hurry.

'Sit down.' May righted a chair that had fallen over before attempting to rub warmth into Rebecca's lifeless hands.

Picking up a towel draped over the washbasin in the corner of the office, she dried Rebecca's dripping hair. The rain had turned it such a deep rust May almost expected it to stain the towel.

'Can you tell me what happened?' she coaxed, unsure if Rebecca's cheeks were wet from the rain or tears.

'*Incidente,*' Rebecca said.

'There's been an accident?'

Rebecca did not respond.

'On the track?' May persisted with her interrogation.

'My mother.' Rebecca's voice was a hoarse croak.

'Florence was involved?' A quiver of alarm jolted May's spine.

'She skid into barrier.'

'Here, drink this,' May poured out some coffee from the percolator and cupping Rebecca's hands around the mug raised it to her lips.

Like a docile child Rebecca swallowed a mouthful of the liquid.

'There, that's better,' May soothed, relieved when some colour returned to her pale cheeks.

A shadow moved in the doorway behind her. Vin gestured to May to join him in the corridor.

'I can't get much sense out of Rebecca,' she confided.

Vin's overalls dripped water on to the floor, encircling his feet in dark puddles.

He shook his head, spraying raindrops over May's face. She hardly noticed the discomfort.

'Florence and Rebecca argued,' he explained.

'Do you know what it was about?'

'It was Rebecca who drained my fuel tank.'

'Why?'

'I don't know.'

'What's happened to Florence?'

'She accosted me, saying she wanted to do the test drive on one of our high performance cars. She's a difficult person to cross especially when she's in one of her moods and before I could say anything she'd snatched the keys off their hook on the wall.

'She took the horseshoe bend too fast and with the wet conditions the car spun out of control and hit the barrier. She's concussed and they're taking her to hospital for a check-up.'

'Is there anything I can do?'

'Can you look after Rebecca until her grandmother arrives?'

May glanced over her shoulder. Rebecca had not moved.

'Where's Auguste?' she asked.

'He wanted to remain on site but the doctor insisted he return to the villa. There's nothing he can do here and he wasn't looking well. I think the shock resurrected memories of Hector's accident.' A bleeper requested Vin's presence on the circuit. 'I have to go.'

He leaned forward and brushed May's cheek with a brief kiss. In the distance an emergency siren shattered the silence.

'You'd better go and find out what's going on,' May urged, her face wet from where Vin's hair had grazed her cheek. 'I'll take care of Rebecca.'

'Thank you,' he said again before striding off down the corridor.

'I am so sorry,' Rebecca hiccuped. She was still clutching her coffee mug. May prised it out of her fingers and placed it on the shelf behind her.

'It doesn't matter,' she assured Rebecca.

'I'm cold.' She shivered.

Wishing she had something for shock,

May continued rubbing her hair as dry as she could manage on the small hand towel.

'My mother isn't dead, is she?'

'No.'

'Is that what Vin came to tell you?'

'Florence is fine,' May reassured her, 'but they need to do a check-up.'

'What were you and Vin whispering about in the corridor?'

'We're to stay here until your grandmother arrives.'

Rebecca grasped May's hand.

'You may not want to stay with me when I tell you what I have done.'

'Try me.' May smiled encouragingly.

'I wanted you to break down in the car, not Vin. I took the petrol and I told Nonno Lombardi you had stayed out all night. I was jealous. Vin likes you more than he likes me. My mother was cross. We argued.'

'I think I can live with that,' May assured Rebecca.

'And you don't hate me?'

May pushed the girl's damp hair away

172

from her face and looked into her troubled brown eyes.

'I don't hate you,' she assured her, 'and I'd like us to be friends, so why don't we start again?'

'Nonna!' Rebecca let go of May's hand and jumping to her feet ran towards her grandmother.

May rose to her feet in shock.

'Betta?'

'What has been happening here?' Betta demanded, her dark eyes aflame with anger.

'You're Rebecca's grandmother?'

'Vin said there has been an accident.'

'Florence's car spun on the horseshoe bend.'

'Is this your doing?' she accused May.

'No, I was with Auguste when it happened.'

'Why my daughter has to prove herself like this I do not know. She should leave car driving to the men. How badly hurt is she?'

'She has been taken to the hospital for a check-up.'

Betta looked unconvinced by May's explanation.

'And what have you been doing to distress Rebecca?'

'The accident was my fault,' Rebecca began sobbing again, 'and I have upset Nonno Lombardi, too.'

Betta muttered something unintelligible under her breath and cradled her granddaughter to her bosom.

'It is always the same with those Lombardis. They cause all the trouble. The Gemelli girls, too; you and your mother and her friend.'

Stunned into temporary silence, May watched Betta console her sobbing granddaughter.

'I'm sorry,' she apologised in a quiet voice, not wanting to further distress Rebecca.

'Your mother had the sense to stay away. Why did you have to come stirring things up?'

'Nonna, please,' Rebecca implored, 'can we go home?'

'Of course, my angel.' Betta turned

her back on May and without a further glance in her direction put her arm around her granddaughter's shoulders. 'First we go home then we visit the hospital.'

The thunder rumbled a reminder that the storm wasn't completely over as Betta opened the office door and led her weeping granddaughter out of the office and down the stairs towards the exit.

Unexpected Promise

'You had no right opening an invitation addressed to me.' Tish looked so angry on the screen May knocked over a padded velvet stool as she took a step backwards away from her dressing table. After checking up on Auguste and being assured by his housekeeper he was resting and quite comfortable and that she would contact May immediately if there was any change in his condition she decided she could no longer put off contacting her mother.

'I always deal with your mail when you're away,' she replied in an attempt to justify her action.

'Anything personal you know you should forward to me.'

'Tish . . . ' May began.

'Perhaps it's time you started calling me Mother,' Tish responded in a cold voice, her aquamarine eyes glinting in anger.

She no longer looked like the fun-loving older sister she often pretended to be when the two of them were out together.

May, too, was now growing angry.

'And perhaps it's time you told me about my other parent, my father, or had you forgotten he existed?'

The familiar shuttered look came over Tish's face.

'Is that what this is all about — your father?'

'In a way. I knew you'd never tell me about him so I decided to take things into my own hands.'

'I told you you were born in Milan.'

'Because you had to — but you've never told me anything else.'

'You don't need to know anything else.'

'Are you ashamed of my father?'

'No.' Tish screwed up her face in anguish.

'Why won't you tell me about him?'

It was a conversation they had had many times before but Tish had remained resolutely silent on the subject.

'I can't,' she said in a hollow voice, lowering her gaze.

May expelled a deep sigh.

'Can I ask questions?'

'Why couldn't you leave well alone?' Tish's reply came out as a low moan.

'Am I Hector Lombardi's daughter?'

Tish's eyes snapped back to the screen.

'You've met Auguste?'

'Of course I've met him.'

'Did he say anything?'

'About what?'

Tish shrugged.

'I don't know.'

'If you mean the earrings, just about everyone has commented on them. Why didn't you tell me they were real?'

'They're not.' A look of panic crossed Tish's face.

'Don't fib.'

A solitary tear trickled down Tish's face. She scrubbed it away with the back of her hand.

'You don't understand,' she said quietly.

'Well, explain, then.'

'It was all so long ago . . . ' Tish's

voice faded away and she looked lost in thought. 'I can't do this.'

May decided it was time to jerk her mother into action.

'I have some news for you. It may change your mind.'

Tish's head shot up.

'What?'

'It's about Florence.'

'What about her?'

'She's had an accident.'

Tish sagged against her desk.

'Tish . . . Mother,' May began.

'I'm all right,' she insisted, flapping a hand in the direction of her screen, 'and I didn't mean what I said. Call me Tish. What's happened to Florence?'

'The car she was driving at the auto-dromo spun out of control.'

'She's not dead?'

'She's in hospital.'

'Will she live?'

'I'm sorry. I didn't mean to break the news to you like this.' May took pity on her mother. 'She's concussed but other-wise she's fine.'

May's alarm deepened. Her mother really didn't look well. A silence fell between them. Tish sipped water and attempted a frail smile.

'It's all been such a shock,' she admitted, 'coming home and finding you weren't here. I contacted Archie Fisher and he told me the two of you had split and he had no idea were you were. I haven't dared tell your grandmother about any of this.'

'How is Coco?' May's conscience pricked her. Her grandmother had always been the sensitive one in the family.

'I've left her in Melbourne,' Tish replied.

'She didn't come back with you?'

'She's having such a good time I didn't see the need. Besides, I had to fly home at short notice when Head Office recalled me.'

'Your meeting.' May had forgotten about it. 'What happened?'

Tish took a deep breath.

'Bookings are down. The market is

going through a tough time. Cutbacks are necessary. I was a victim of the cutbacks.'

'Run that past me again.' May wasn't sure she had heard Tish correctly.

'I've lost my job,' Tish replied in a slow voice.

The colour drained from May's face as she looked at her mother.

'They can't do that to you.'

'They can and they have — effective immediately.'

'You're out of work?'

'You've got it in one.'

'What are you doing to do?'

'I'll survive. I have contacts in the business. It's time to call in some favours,' Tish replied with a trace of her old self.

'If nothing comes up I can always go out on the road again. Don't worry about me.'

'Coco's not stranded in Australia, is she?'

'No, she's staying on there for a while. She likes the lifestyle and it's helping her recovery. She's rooming with a friend so no issues there and she can come home any time she likes. I made sure she had an open air ticket.'

Tish attempted another smile but it didn't quite work. May suspected her nerves were in shreds. Like most artists she had a fragile ego and the loss of her job would have been a severe body blow.

'Would you like me to come home?' May offered. 'Right now I'm not popular around here, I've been stirring up old memories. I don't think anyone would be too worried if I left.'

May pushed all thoughts of Vin Piace to the back of her mind. Her mother came first.

'No, don't come home.'

'Why not? You didn't want me coming out here in the first place, rooting around in your past. I've offered you the perfect get out.'

'Perhaps you're right,' Tish acknowledged. 'The time for secrets is over.'

'You mean . . . ' May swallowed. 'What exactly do you mean?'

'I'm coming out to see you.'

'When?'

'I'll be on the first available flight and,' Tish added before she ended the call, 'I promise I'll tell you everything.'

Cancelled Celebrations

rip and before she got to the call. 'I promise I'll tell you everything.'

With her head spinning, May didn't immediately realise someone was knocking on her door.

Vin's muffled voice sounded urgent.

'May, are you there? Open up.' His face was covered in oily streaks and his eyes were etched with fatigue. He sagged against the doorway as if he were about to pass out.

Supporting his weight under her shoulders May staggered into the studio. Vin collapsed on to a chair and cradled his head in his hands. Hurrying into the kitchen she poured some water into a glass.

She held the tumbler steady as she passed it over.

'No, don't speak,' she cautioned.

'Thank you.' Vin wiped his mouth with the back of his hand.

May put the glass down on the table with her right hand, aware Vin was still clutching her left hand. Gently easing her fingers out of his grasp, she perched on the chair next to him.

'Can you update me?' she asked in as steady a voice as she could manage.

'I don't know how it could have happened.' Vin was still shaking his head.

'You're talking about the accident?'

He nodded absently as if his mind were elsewhere.

'It wasn't your fault,' May tried to reassure him. 'Florence's argument with Rebecca would have seriously unsettled her and she wasn't paying full attention to the conditions. She should have known better than to go out on the circuit.'

'She is such a careful driver. She never takes professional risks.'

'The storm would have made the circuit extra slippery — the accident was a force of nature.'

'Do you think so?' Vin turned a hopeful face towards her.

Earlier the maid had lowered the blinds in the room. The storm had passed over and now the afternoon sun was painting psychedelic shapes on to Vin's face as it seeped through the slats.

'All mothers and daughters argue.' May recalled her recent experience with Tish. 'This argument had unfortunate consequences.'

'One of the mechanics heard raised voices coming from the office about the time the storm started.'

'All I could get out of Rebecca was that Florence was very angry with her.'

'I should have forcibly taken the keys from Florence, but short of physically attacking her there was nothing I could do.'

'There was nothing anyone could have done, given the circumstances.'

'Her actions might have compromised the future of the autodromo.'

'You're being unnecessarily harsh on Florence,' May tried reasoning with Vin.

'There will have to be endless reports and enquiries. You have no idea how strict the authorities can be in these matters. We could lose our licence or worse still be closed down.'

'I'm sure it won't come to that.'

'Everyone has worked so hard to make the autodromo a success. I can't let it go under.'

'If anyone is to blame it's me,' May insisted.

'How can it possibly be your fault?' Vin demanded with a puzzled frown.

'If I hadn't come out here none of this would have happened.'

'No,' Vin protested, 'the accident was nothing to do with you.'

'Betta would disagree with you.'

'What's Betta got to do with it?'

'No-one told me she is Florence's mother.'

'How did you find out?'

'When she collected Rebecca, she was like a tigress protecting her cubs.'

'What did she say to you?'

'The usual stuff, how my presence here had stirred up old grievances — grievances better left buried in the past. She blames me for everything.'

'If she's looking for someone to blame,

it's Florence.'

'Betta doesn't agree with you.'

'It was Florence who invited you here in the first place.'

'But she didn't invite me, did she? She invited my mother.'

'I'm too tired to argue about it now.' Vin sagged back in his seat.

May could smell the motor oil on his skin. The top studs of his boiler suit were undone and she could see a pulse throbbing at the base of his neck. It required a superhuman effort on her part not to put out her arms and hug him.

'Would you like some coffee?' she asked instead. Vin gave a tired nod. 'Have you eaten anything?'

'I'm not sure,' he admitted.

'I'll rustle up a sandwich. There are a few emergency supplies in the fridge.'

Looking out across the courtyard as she prepared their snack May could see villa life going on as normal. The gardeners were tending to the damage inflicted by the recent storm, collecting up fallen petals and clearing the pathway of damp leaves, their rakes scraping the sodden surface of the walkway. Picking up the tray, May carried it into the small sitting-room. In her absence Vin had made an effort to tidy himself up. He had run a comb through his hair and made liberal use of her lime-scented soap to wash the worst of the oil off his face. She poured out some orange juice and nudged the plate of sandwiches towards him. Vin caught May looking at the stains his hands left on the paper serviettes.

'My fingers look a wreck, don't they?'

'I've seen worse — especially on location.'

'On location,' he repeated thoughtfully. 'Do you do much filming away from home?'

'Not often.' May grimaced, remembering the way she had been casually let go from her last production.

'You don't like what you do for a living?' Vin enquired.

'I did.'

'Would you miss it if you changed career?'

May refused to dwell on what had happened between her and Archie Fisher.

'I sense my life could be at a crossroads and I'm not sure what direction it's going to take.'

'Like our relationship.' Vin's voice was so low May had to lean forward in order to hear what he was saying.

She breathed in deeply, not wanting to have this conversation but knowing it was inevitable.

'If you are suggesting we should develop our relationship, it wouldn't work.'

Vin's next words stunned her.

'You mean because I am the son of a retired police officer?'

'I mean because you come from a traditional Mediterranean family surrounded by an army of aunts and cousins, all doting on each other.'

'It is the same in most communities, isn't it?'

'My grandparents were largely responsible for my upbringing.'

'That is community, isn't it?'

'I grew up treating my mother as an older sister. As for my father's side of the family I am none the wiser as to his identity.'

'Your point is?'

'I don't know who I am.'

'How would you feel if you are related to Auguste Lombardi?' Vin's eyes never left May's face.

'I can't answer that question.'

'Then let me answer it for you. If you are his granddaughter it would place you in a different social class — way above the likes of the son of a retired police officer.'

'Of course it wouldn't.' May felt annoyed that Vin could think such a thing.

'That is the real reason you think a relationship between us wouldn't work, isn't it?'

'No. Why should it make any difference if I am related to Auguste?'

'One day you could inherit my job.'

'That is not going to happen and not what I'm thinking at all.'

'Family comes first.'

'Can we talk about something else?' May pleaded, regretting having opened up her innermost thoughts to Vin.

He picked up his discarded serviette and wiped oil off his fingers in slow rhythmic movements.

'I owe you an apology.' May tried not to stumble over her words.

'You do not need to apologise for being who you are.'

'I'm talking about the Villa Della Pesca. It was wrong of me to suspect you of running out of fuel on purpose.'

'I am glad. Did Rebecca give you a reason why she acted so irresponsibly?'

May felt her face redden.

'She saw me as a threat to her position here.'

'Because she has always treated Auguste as an honorary grandfather and you could be his actual granddaughter?'

'That and other things.'

There was no way May was going to break Rebecca's confidence by telling him the true reason behind the girl's actions.

'Causing someone to break down in the middle of nowhere is a serious matter.'

'She didn't realise how serious or that the situation would take an unexpected turn.'

'How did she find out what happened?'

'Florence visited the studio and I wasn't there. Rebecca was with her.'

'I see.'

'You have to know that Rebecca told Auguste we spent the night away together. He wasn't best pleased. So in a way you could say Rebecca succeeded in discrediting me.'

'What has Auguste been saying?'

'We were having coffee together before the news of the accident broke. He wanted to know why we skipped his garden party and why I didn't come home last night. I tried to explain but he didn't want to listen to what I had to say. He accused me of blackening the family name.'

'Would you like me to talk to him?'

'I think he's got more important things on his mind right now.'

Vin screwed up his paper serviette and dropped it back on to the table.

'We all have,' he agreed.

'Have you heard any more from the hospital?' May asked.

'Florence suffered severe bruising and has broken a bone in her arm. She won't be driving for a while.' Vin frown. 'I'm not sure what the accident will do to her mental state of mind. She lives life on the edge.'

'Could her career at the autodromo be in shreds?'

'That's a decision someone else will have to make. For the moment the circuit is closed. The mechanics are checking all vehicles and making sure their paperwork will stand up to the inevitable stringent enquiries. We need to be prepared for the authorities.'

'Florence won't be prosecuted, will she?'

'Auguste won't want things taken further but I should tell you she has offered her resignation,' Vin replied.

'Driving is her life.'

'It would be a big wrench for her to give it up but maybe it is time to move on. Rebecca's actions sound to me like a cry for help. Mother and daughter need to spend time together away from Bella Acqua.'

'Auguste would be lost without her.'

'I think he too needs space away from Florence and Rebecca. All the recent excitement has proved too much for him.'

'What will happen about the rest of the celebrations?'

'They have been cancelled. Most of the guests have left.'

'We are going to have at least one more guest,' May recalled her conversation with Tish.

'Who?' Vin asked.

'My mother.'

'I thought she was in Australia.' With an exhausted expression on his face Vin leaned back and closed his eyes.

'She's home.' May paused, debating

how to update Vin on the situation with her mother. She glanced at him. His head had fallen forward and he had fallen asleep. May snatched up the ringing telephone before it could disturb Vin.

'Signorina Maxwell? This is the housekeeper. Sr Lombardi would like to see you. Would tomorrow morning at eleven o'clock suit you?'

'I'll be there,' May replied.

Replacing the receiver she went in search of a blanket for Vin.

Guest Appearances

'Good morning.'

May jumped at the sound of Vin's voice behind her.

'What are you doing here?' She spun round. 'I thought you would be tied up with the race track officials all day.'

'I had to clear my head so I left them to it for a while.'

'Have you made any progress?'

'Not that you would notice so I'm here now to make sure nothing disastrous happens to you.'

'I think I can manage the short walk across the gardens on my own.' May hitched her bag over her shoulder and checked she had closed the door properly behind her.

'I'm sure you can but I also want to thank you for your hospitality yesterday and to say I'm sorry I fell asleep on you. It was not polite behaviour.'

'Eating olives, peaches and mozzarella

cheese washed down with red wine is not something I do very often, either,' May admitted.

When Vin had stirred from his deep sleep May had been sitting opposite him catching up on her e-mails. Neither of them felt like eating much supper and not wanting to disturb the kitchen staff, May had salvaged what she could from the small fridge in her kitchenette and the two of them had settled on the sofa, sharing plates of cheese and olives and glasses of red wine.

'It was the best supper I've had in a long time but don't tell my mother. She prides herself on her cooking.'

Later after Vin had left, May relaxed in a scented bath before slipping between the fresh cotton sheets of her large double bed. The lingering aroma of the sweet orange oil sent her into a deep and dreamless sleep, which wasn't disturbed until one of the maids delivered a morning tray of tea.

Uncertain what to wear for her forthcoming meeting with Auguste she had opted for traditional casual and chosen a button-through dress of pale green cheesecloth, a long-time favourite of hers and one she felt comfortable wearing. The housekeeper had assured her that Auguste had passed a restful night and was looking forward to seeing her.

'Have you spoken to Auguste since the accident?' May asked as they headed towards the pathway leading to the camellia garden.

Vin shook his head.

'I couldn't get past his housekeeper.'

He fell into step beside May as they crossed the freshly clipped lawn and strolled in the direction of the villa. More leaves had fallen in the night and the gardeners were hard at work clearing up the debris.

The tang of fresh lemons drifted over from the small orchard on the south side of the garden. May hoped the trees had been sturdy enough to withstand the strength of yesterday's storm and the fallen fruit wouldn't lie rotting and unforgotten on the grass.

She momentarily closed her eyes in an attempt to commit all the sights and sounds and smells of the villa to memory. This could possibly be her last day in Bella Acqua and she didn't want to forget a thing.

'What time do you think she will arrive?' Vin asked.

May paused.

'It's difficult to say. She can be unpredictable.'

'You don't think she'll turn up?'

'She was annoyed over what I'd done and I don't think she wanted to return to Bella Acqua, but for some reason she had a change of heart.'

'It must have been a big decision for her.'

'I'm sure we'll see her — sooner or later.'

'I know very little about her despite all the rumours and gossip. What is she really like?'

'It's difficult to know where to start. When I was a child she would host impromptu parties. Mothers would come to our house expecting to collect their children and find Tish had taken us all off for a skate boarding session or a ride on a roller coaster.

'My grandparents were always making excuses for her. She loved a good protest too. If something didn't please her she didn't hesitate to stir up local officials. The mayor used to hide from her whenever he saw her coming.' The ghost of a smile hovered on May's lips.

'She was very different from other people's mothers. That's why it's so difficult to be cross with her for long. I just wish she had told me more about her past,' May added wistfully. 'None of this would have been necessary if she had.'

'You love her very much, don't you?' Vin spoke in a soft voice.

'Of course I do but before I came out here I didn't understand what motivated her.'

'And now you do?'

'I have a better idea of what she went through with Lis and Florence and why she's always challenged authority but

I can't believe she would go as far as breaking the law. She's not a thief.'

In the distance the sound of a car revving up on the autodromo circuit disturbed the butterflies sunning themselves in the wild.flower garden.

'Looks like we're in action again,' Vin said.

May jerked herself back to the present.

'Have the authorities finished their enquiries already?'

'They haven't officially started them.'

'Perhaps you should go and find out what's happening.'

'We have been granted a provisional licence so I don't think there's any infringement of regulations going on. I don't know how Florence did it but she has charmed the safety marshal into verifying her version of events.

'She told him she skidded on an earlier oil spill and that caused the accident and he's allowed us to carry on with our routine activities on a temporary basis. Auguste has a good local reputation and

Florence used that to argue her case.'

'Surely she hasn't been interviewed already.'

'She insisted on it.'

'In hospital?'

'She's home. She discharged herself and she was on the telephone to the authorities first thing this morning.'

They paused by the steps leading up to the front entrance of the villa.

'Want me to come in with you?' Vin enquired.

'Perhaps I'd better go in alone,' May decided. 'I wouldn't want to overtire Auguste.'

'I should get back to the autodromo,' Vin conceded, 'and see what's going on.'

'If you see Florence, give her my best wishes.'

'Talking of Florence, it looks like she needs me urgently.' Vin scanned an incoming message. 'I hope she hasn't done anything rash. You know where to find me if you need me.'

Vin touched May's arm in a gesture of support. May stayed where she was until he reached the iron gates leading on to the main road and she heard him drive off before she mounted the stone steps up to the main entrance to the villa.

'Sr Lombardi is waiting for you, signorina,' the housekeeper greeted her and led May through to the terrace.

Although it was a warm morning Auguste had a rug wrapped around his knees and wore a jumper.

'I've thrown off the shawl,' he confided. 'My housekeeper is of the opinion I'll freeze to death out here and without Florence around to keep an eye on me she has taken on the role of carer with enthusiasm.' He held out his arms for an embrace.

'I am sorry I was too tired to see you earlier. Tell me the latest.'

May perched on the edge of a sun chair, uncertain where to start.

'I know very little,' she admitted.

'Didn't I see you walking across the garden with Vin Piace?'

'He came to see if I wanted company,' she explained.

'I see you don't,' Auguste replied.

'I didn't think you would want too many visitors.'

'You're right, I don't — and Vin will have more than enough to do dealing with the authorities.

'I am embarrassed to have caused such a fuss yesterday and you can reassure Vin the next time I see him I won't interfere or start breathing down his neck demanding to know what is going on.'

Auguste seemed more like his old self, no longer annoyed with her and happy to sit and talk about recent events.

'You know the remainder of the festivities have been cancelled? I can't say I'm sorry. I went along with Florence's plans to celebrate my birthday because I didn't want to hurt her feelings but,' Auguste leaned forward in a gesture of confidentiality, 'I'm glad they've been cut short.'

'How are you feeling this morning?' May noted he had more colour in his cheeks.

'Rested, but my doctor says I have to take things easy for a day or two. From the noise in the background I assume there is activity over at the autodromo.'

'Vin's gone back to keep an eye on things.'

'Perhaps you would be kind enough to pour out some water for me,' Auguste asked.

May added some slices of fresh lemon to the drinks.

'Thank you.' Auguste drank half the contents of his glass before replacing it on the small table beside his chair.

'I'm not tiring you, am I?' May asked. 'Would you like me to come back later?'

Auguste sipped some more of his water.

'You have something else you would rather be doing?'

'No.' May gave a flustered denial, knowing how easy it had been in the past to upset Auguste and hoping she hadn't said the wrong thing.

'Then you must stay and talk to me.'

May couldn't help wondering where

their meeting was going. She was convinced Auguste hadn't asked her over merely to pass the time of day.

'The storm has done significant damage to the trellises, so my head gardener tells me,' Auguste said.

She stirred the ice cubes in her glass with a swizzle stick. Aware Auguste was subjecting her to a look of intense scrutiny, she couldn't help wishing he would give some indication as to the reason for this summons.

'A while ago if you can recall we were talking about earrings, weren't we?' he asked as if reading May's mind. 'Before other events got in the way.'

She nodded.

'If I tell you the history of the earrings will you promise not to over-react?'

'As long as you promise not to have me arrested.' May spoke in a steady voice trying to control the rapid beating of her heart.

'Why would I want to have you arrested?'

'Because we both know they are not

mine.'

'They were given to you and you should enjoy wearing them.'

'I can't, unless,' May looked hopefully at Auguste, 'you are going to tell me they really are coloured glass.'

'I'm afraid not. They are genuine emeralds.'

'Are you absolutely certain?'

'I am. You see, they belonged to my wife.'

'It's true? They are part of the Lombardi collection?' May sat bolt upright.

'Yes.'

'You must have them back,' May insisted.

'What use are they to me? Jewellery should be worn, not hidden away. I want you to keep them and wear them.'

'That doesn't seem right.'

'It does to me. Think of them as a gift. Hector gave them to your mother and she passed them on to you.'

'Do you have any idea why your son gave them to my mother?'

'I wish I did but,' Auguste paused,

'no, I don't. I think I told you we weren't close?'

May nodded.

'But enough about Hector — I can see from the expression on your face there is something else worrying you. Would you like to share it with me?'

'It's my mother. I have been in contact with her.'

'In Australia?'

'She was there but she isn't any more.'

May was distracted by the sound of footsteps approaching from the far corner of the terrace. She turned in their direction.

'Who on earth can this be? I told the housekeeper I didn't want any more visitors.'

Two women rounded the corner.

'Not even me?' one of them asked in a teasing voice.

'My dear,' Auguste broke into a smile, 'I am always pleased to see you.'

'And what's more, Auguste, I've brought an old friend with me.'

May leaped to Auguste's side as he

struggled to his feet.

'Am I seeing things?' His face was wreathed in a huge smile.

'Hello, Auguste,' the second woman greeted him, 'it's good to see you again.'

'Welcome to the Villa Lombardi,' he said before enveloping her in a huge hug.

End of Story?

Sofia Napoli was wearing a chic crushed raspberry dress and matching jacket but she looked far from confident as her blue eyes darted from Auguste to May and back to Auguste. The woman who had stepped back from hugging Auguste and was now standing at her side presented a more challenging image in black leggings, a rock chick logo T-shirt and a scarlet bandeau entwined round her mop of chestnut curls. Her eyes were full of fire.

'I should be so angry with you,' Tish's blue green eyes flashed at her daughter then softened into a smile, 'but you've reunited me with my old friend and I am the last one in the world to blame anyone for being an activist, so thank you, my darling. Come here and give me a kiss.'

'Old friend?' May echoed.

'Haven't you worked it out yet?' she

teased and drew Sofia into the embrace. 'Signora Napoli, who in my day was known as Lis Gilbert, is the other half of The Beautiful Twins.'

The scales fell from May's eyes as her mouth fell open in surprise. Why hadn't she guessed? Sofia Napoli had more or less told her who she was, but May had been so wrapped up in investigating her mother's past she hadn't picked up on the clues Sofia had dripped in her direction.

'I tried to tell you,' Sofia took up the story, 'but when I realised you knew nothing about me, I chickened out.'

'Coward.' Tish dug her in the ribs with her elbow.

'Not at all,' Sofia objected. 'Your mother and I did not part on good terms,' she confided to May, 'And I didn't want to stir up old grievances.'

'All forgotten now.' Tish hugged her friend.

'You're the one who went missing.' May spoke in a faint voice.

'I didn't go missing.' Sophie bridled.

'I reinvented myself.'

'She always was a survivor.' Tish's eyes danced with amusement.

'You haven't changed, either,' Sofia protested. 'Look at you, still dressed like a hippy.'

The two women exchanged an indulgent look.

'Did you know about this?' May quizzed Auguste.

'It's beyond my wildest dreams,' he replied, a smile of pure pleasure on his face.

'Is that a yes or a no?'

'May, stop teasing Auguste,' Sofia chided. 'He knew nothing. Neither did I until I got Florence's call.'

'It's a story we will save for another time.' Tish was still looking at her daughter. 'Right now what matters is I'm here and,' she tossed her head, 'I hope I am forgiven.'

'What for?'

May saw regret and sadness in her mother's mesmerising eyes.

'Because I didn't tell you about my

past.' A fleeting look of uncertainty crossed Tish's face. 'You see, I thought you wouldn't love me quite so much if you knew the truth and I don't think I could have lived with that.'

'What?' May gasped.

'Exactly,' Sofia chimed in. 'You've said some stupid things in your time, Tish, but this about beats them all. You have a beautiful daughter. Of course she loves you. She'll always love you no matter what you've done — which isn't much, I would add.'

'Come here.' Tish trembled in her arms as May gave her a fierce hug. 'You really were scared about coming back, weren't you?'

'You have no idea.' Tish's generous lips curved into a shaky smile. 'All this,' she indicated the head band and the T-shirt, 'is a front.'

'But you're one of the bravest people I know. You've taken on half the town's dignitaries and come out on top.'

Tish's aquamarine eyes regained some of their sparkle.

'Are you saying everything's still OK between us?'

'You don't even have to ask.'

Sofia sighed then clapped her hands.

'What did I tell you? Now explanations, come on, Tish, there's no time like the present.'

'You go first,' she insisted, still clinging on to May.

'Right,' Sofia straightened her shoulders, 'to start with, I adopted my middle name of Lis and I don't know why I chose Gilbert,' she admitted. 'My given name was Strom, maybe I thought it sounded too much like storm. Whatever.'

'She's half Norwegian,' Tish confided to May. 'That's why she's got such lovely blonde hair.'

'My mother was Italian and we were visiting my grandmother when I met Tish in the market trying to charm a free peach off a stallholder.'

'I was working my way across Europe with friends and somehow I lost them,' Tish explained.

'Why doesn't that surprise me?' May

raised tolerant eyebrows.

'I'd also lost my backpack. I had nothing. Lis came to my rescue.'

'I lent her money to buy her peach — a loan which was never repaid,' Sofia pointed out with a light laugh.

'After that Lis and I palled up. She was at a loose end so we started singing. It started as a joke but things took off. Before we knew it we were in big demand.'

'Why didn't you keep in touch with each other after the group split?' May demanded.

An uneasy glance passed between the two older women, neither of whom seemed eager to carry on with their explanation.

'What caused the big fall out?' May tried another question. 'And why the secrecy? Was it because you really were the jewel thieves?'

'No, we were not!' Sofia's voice rose in outrage. 'How could you think such a thing?'

'Until someone tells me the truth I

don't know what to think.'

'Ah, Maria,' Auguste addressed the housekeeper who hearing the sound of voices had presented herself on the terrace, 'some refreshments for our guests, if you would be so kind.'

'Certainly, Signore.'

'You know,' Tish leaned towards Lis, 'we should do another gig.'

'To celebrate Auguste's birthday? What a good idea.'

'We'd show your generation a thing or two.' Tish did an experimental wriggle of her hips.

'I've put on a few pounds,' Sofia confessed, 'and I don't sing so much these days.'

'You'd soon get back into the swing of things.'

'Is anyone going to tell me the end of the story?' May demanded.

'Sorry, darling. Where were we?'

'I always wanted a daughter,' Sofia sounded sad as she looked at May and Tish, 'but I never had children.'

'You can have a share in mine if you

like. I'm sure May wouldn't mind.'

Sofia reached out and stroked May's hair.

'You are so beautiful, May. I immediately saw the resemblance to your mother.'

'Careful. May doesn't do being told she's beautiful,' Tish interrupted. 'She's very today, you know hashtags and no gender stereotyping.'

'Goodness,' Sofia recoiled, 'I see you have a thing or two to teach me about modern manners.'

'And there are things you can teach us, Lis,' Tish insisted. 'All about your charity work. She helps youngsters develop literacy skills and loads of other stuff,' she explained to May.

'You know it must be years since anyone's called me Lis.' A dreamy look came into Sofia's eyes.

'If there's one thing age teaches you it is patience.' Auguste patted May's hand as her frustration threatened to get the better of her. 'They'll get round to us eventually and you wouldn't deny them their little reunion, would you?'

Sofia settled down next to May.

'I'm sorry. Here we are talking about old times when you must be bursting with curiosity. You wanted to know why we didn't keep in touch.'

'In your own time.' May realised she would get nowhere if she tried to hurry Sofia along.

'At school I was always getting into trouble for talking too much, so after the robberies I decided to keep quiet and to lie low, but over the years what happened has weighed heavily on my mind. I can't tell you how pleased I am it's all coming out in the open now.' Sofia stroked May's arm.

'Darling,' Tish sat down on the other side of May, 'you have no idea how often I too battled with my conscience. I wanted to get it all off my chest but I didn't know how to start.

'It was as though I had two separate lives, a before and after, and the two didn't match up.'

'Do you remember the fun we had

doing the before bit?' Sofia leaned across May, her face alight with laughter.

'It wasn't all fun,' Tish contradicted. 'Changing into flimsy costumes in the back of a draughty vehicle or losing precious make-up because in a fit of pique someone left it in the ladies' room.'

'That wasn't me.' Sofia looked deceptively innocent.

'Yes, it was. You could be a right little madam at times.'

'Florence was the worst,' Sofia declared.

'Don't dish the dirt on her, she's not here to defend herself and you know we were as bad as each other.'

'I never told Franco the half of it,' Sofia confided, 'and I never will. These days I have a social status to uphold.'

Tish exploded into a bout of unladylike laughter. Sofia glared at her before allowing a smile to creep across her face and she too broke into uncontrollable laughter. Auguste, who had maintained a dignified silence, sighed heavily.

'The older generation are supposed to

set a good example to today's youth,' he cautioned.

'You weren't exactly a role model in your earlier days,' Sofia batted back. 'Sorry,' she backtracked with her winsome smile, 'you have every reason to be proud of all you have done with the autodromo and the young people you sponsor.'

'Your refreshments, sir.' A housemaid created a welcome interruption.

'Is Vin Piace Alberto Piace's son?' Tish asked as they sorted out cups and plates.

'You've met Vin?' May could not disguise her surprise.

'He collected me from the airport.'

'When?'

'After my flight landed, of course, May, do try to keep up.'

'Then he picked me up from the station,' Sofia butted in, 'and in answer to your question, Tish, Vin is Alberto Piace's son.'

'He seemed to know all about me.'

'Vin is Auguste's right-hand man.'

Tish helped herself to another sandwich and a handful of mixed nuts.

'How do you stay so thin?' Sofia demanded.

'Because I lead a full and challenging life — you should try it some time.' 'I'll have you know my days are full, thank you very much.'

May turned her head from side to side trying to keep up with the speed of their banter.

'How did Vin know which flight you were on?' she interrupted.

'Florence told him.'

'How did Florence know?'

'I told her.'

'You contacted Florence?'

'Now you're getting the hang of it.' Tish beamed at her. 'These mini prawns in pasta are seriously good.' She turned back to the spread on the coffee table in front of her.

'And have you tried those little lemon puffs? They are as light as air.' Sofia put a couple on her plate.

'Why doesn't everyone eat first?' Auguste suggested. 'May, did you have any breakfast?'

'A cup of tea.'

'You have to eat.' Tish looked appalled by this piece of news. 'Everything will seem much better on a full stomach and you might not be so cross with me afterwards.'

'Auguste.' Sofia offered him a plate of peach flans. 'Would you like one of these?'

'Thank you, no,' he declined. 'My pleasure is to play the host. You know, this is the best of my birthday celebrations,' he added. 'All I have to do is look at the three of you enjoying yourselves and I'm happy.'

Tish eventually leaned back with a satisfied sigh as Sofia brushed pastry crumbs off her elegant costume and dabbed her lips.

'Now come on out with it, Lis, time to 'fess up,' Tish insisted. 'Poor May must be bursting with curiosity.'

'I don't know where to start,' Sofia admitted.

'I'll start you off,' Auguste said. Sofia tensed but gave him a brief nod of encouragement. 'How did my wife's emeralds come to be in May's possession?'

A deadly silence fell between Tish and Sofia.

'Go on.' Tish squeezed her friend's hands. 'I'm right with you.'

'I hid them in Tish's bag,' Sofia mumbled, looking down at the ground.

Auguste leaned forward.

'Why did you do that?' he asked calmly.

'No excuse, I panicked. I thought if they were found in my possession I would have been suspected of their theft.'

'So you shifted the blame on to your friend?' Auguste continued with his line of questioning.

'I had to.' Sofia looked as though her action was the most natural thing in the world. 'I was the main culprit. You see, loads of people heard me admiring the earrings. They couldn't have known Hector would give them to me.'

'Hector gave them to you?' May repeated.

'It's not a very good explanation, is it, even though it's true?'

'She was so very beautiful,' Tish

sighed, 'and Hector was smitten.'

'I'm not proud of what I did.' Sofia lowered her eyes back to the ground. 'It's the way I was in those days.'

'When did you find out what Sofia had done?' May asked her mother.

'I didn't at first. But Florence caught her in the act and she told Betta, and Betta was scared Andreas might lose his position with Auguste so she reported their loss to the police.

'We were young and frightened. We thought we might be sent to jail for something we hadn't done and we didn't steal any jewels, no matter what Alberto Piace thought.' Two bright pink spots of colour stained Sofia's cheeks.

'And so you ran away,' May said.

'Franco was always asking me to marry him, so we eloped.'

'And I fled to Milan, taking the earrings with me,' Tish added. 'I know I should have given them back to you, Auguste, but I didn't know how to without arousing suspicion.'

'Florence and I vowed never to talk

225

of the matter again,' Sofia said, 'and we rarely met up — Florence blamed me for what happened. She was right. It was my fault.'

'Actually . . . ' Auguste's interruption made everyone jump. 'Andreas knew the identity of the jewel thieves.'

'Why didn't Florence tell us?' Sofia reacted with indignation.

'Because she didn't know.'

'Hang on,' Tish interrupted. 'Footnotes needed here.'

'Do you remember the man Andreas used to work for?' Auguste asked.

Tish frowned.

'I may have seen him once or twice lurking around in the background.'

'He employed a group of young men to cover his activities, the ones who used to follow you girls around.'

'You mean it was our fault all along?' Tish's eyebrows met her headband.

'You were targeted,' Auguste replied. 'Andreas suspected what was going on. That's why he wanted out. When his application for a job at the autodromo was successful he proposed to Florence and came to work for me.

'After Hector's accident I voiced my suspicions to the police.'

'About the time we all disappeared,' Tish said.

'No wonder gossip was rife,' Sofia agreed.

'We were so scared,' Tish said in a sad voice. 'I mean, who would have believed us?'

'Why didn't the police clear our names if they knew we were innocent?' Sofia demanded.

'They didn't actually accuse you of anything,' Auguste pointed out. 'As only a handful of the jewels were recovered, the files were eventually closed. End of story.'

'We have to tell Florence the good news,' Sofia announced. 'After all these years we have been proved innocent.'

'She is still recovering from her accident,' Auguste cautioned.

'In that case I suspect she will be ten times more difficult than usual. Sparks will fly,' Sofia predicted.

'I can't wait to see her again after all these years.' Tish leaped to her feet.

'Please . . . ' May grabbed hold of her elbow before she could take off with Sofia. 'I need to know one more thing.'

'Darling.' Tish turned back. 'Have I missed something out?'

'The most important part of your story.' May took a deep breath. 'Was Hector Lombardi my father?'

The Truth is Out

'So you thought to put some water between me and my mother?'

May and Vin sat on the deck of the floating restaurant. Beneath them, the fairy lights cast bright colours on to the rippling water gently lapping the hull.

'It seemed the safest course of action and what we have to say to each other is too important for interruptions.'

Vin looked unusually serious and May hadn't felt this nervous since her last audition. If Vin didn't agree to her proposal this could possibly be their last meeting.

'Your mother and her friends are creating havoc in Bella Acqua. All their old admirers are out in force. Everyone is loving it, and as for the gossipmongers, they are having a field day.'

'You know they've decided to go on a short holiday? Florence is still downhearted after her accident and they thought a mini break would help them re-bond.'

'Florence has had a tough time of it recently. The locals were worried that the autodromo might remain permanently closed and several of the employees blamed her.'

'But it's open again now?'

'Enquiries are still pending but it's only a matter of formality. So where are the three of them off to on this mini-break?'

'Contessa Rosamunde has offered the use of the Villa Della Pesca. They decided they have a lot of history to get through and Florence can convalesce away from Betta and Rebecca.'

'That is a good idea. Everyone's been on edge since the accident. They need time to chill.'

Vin cast May a guarded look as they lapsed into silence. Over the past few days May had seen little of him. Tish with her usual whirlwind enthusiasm had insisted on revisiting her old haunts.

Auguste had provided a car and driver and together she and May had toured the area with Sofia.

The fairy lights cast shadows on the dark circles under Vin's eyes. May heard he had been working round the clock to ensure the continued running of the autodromo and without Florence's assistance it hadn't been easy.

'I have decided on a career change,' May blurted out before her nerve failed her.

'You are giving up acting?'

'I lost out on my last role to the producer's niece and I expect it will happen again.' May gave a rueful smile. 'I'm beginning to understand what motivated my mother to give up singing.'

'I don't follow.' Vin appeared confused.

'Always changing into costume in less than ideal conditions, working seriously unsocial hours, the glamour soon wears off.'

'What have you got in mind?' The tone of Vin's voice was not encouraging.

'I have an idea and I'd like to run it past you.'

'Is this anything to do with Auguste?'

'In a way. You know he's retiring from the business with immediate effect?'

Vin nodded but said nothing. May had rehearsed what she was going to say but she knew breaking the news to Vin wouldn't be easy.

'Florence's accident unsettled him and when he found out what Rebecca had been up to he decided the autodromo wasn't a good influence on her so he's arranged that she should go to Milan to study fashion. Florence has indicated she would like to move there, too.'

'Perhaps a complete break would be a good thing for everyone. And this idea of yours is?' Vin prompted.

'I don't know if you are going to like it.'

'You don't have to break the news gently,' Vin insisted. 'I can guess what you are going to say.'

May blinked.

'I didn't think telling you would prove

this difficult.'

'Let me help you out,' Vin offered. 'It's rather like your producer and his niece, isn't it?'

The noisy celebrations of a group of diners at a neighbouring table weren't helping May's concentration.

'What do you mean?'

'It's not what you know, it's who you know or who you are related to. I presume your new job will be at the autodromo.'

'Is that such a bad idea?'

'As a filing clerk, no, but you're talking about taking over from Auguste. There's a big difference.'

'No, that's not what I'm talking about.'

'And you want me to play nursemaid?'

'We seem to have got our wires crossed.'

'Before you offer me the job of second in command I'm turning it down.'

'Vin, will you listen?' May raised her voice.

'If Auguste chooses to put his grand-daughter in charge of the autodromo then I wish the pair of you good luck.

I'm not sure how you'll manage without Florence or myself but that's not my problem. Now was there anything else?'

May fixed her eyes on Vin's.

'Auguste Lombardi is not my grandfather.'

Vin didn't move a muscle.

'Did you hear what I said?'

Vin remained silent.

'And I have no intention of taking over his job at the autodromo — or yours, come to that.'

'If you're not going to inherit the business who is going to take over?' Vin demanded.

'I can guess who Auguste has in mind, but he hasn't confided in me.'

Vin filled his glass with water and drank the contents before speaking again.

'I jumped to conclusions,' he admitted.

'The wrong ones,' May reminded him.

'What was it you wanted to tell me?' he asked. Vin's attention strayed to the view across the lake and May knew she had precious little time to get her proposal across.

'First of all I would like to tell you about my father.'

'Go ahead,' Vin said in a toneless voice.

'He was descended from Italian nobility. His family did not approve of his relationship with my mother. A penniless English girl who performed on stage for her living was not what they had in mind for their son.

'When they found out what was going on they sent him off to visit relatives in America. Before he went he married my mother in secret and gave her some money, promising to send for her as soon as he could.

'She gave birth to me in Milan but heard nothing more from my father. She waited as long as she could before the money ran out and she was forced to return to England.'

Vin slowly turned his attention back to May.

'Tish dropped her stage name of Delacourt and adopted a new name, Maxwell,' May continued, 'in order to cover her tracks because she was worried my father's family would come looking for her.

'She also feared the authorities might start asking awkward questions and link her sudden disappearance as an admission of guilt.'

'We're back to the jewel robberies again, are we?'

'It was a very traumatic time for her. There was no way she could check up on her husband and she didn't dare tell anyone she was married.'

'So no-one ever knew about him?'

'Eventually she received notification from an American law firm. Somehow they had managed to track her down. They informed her that my father had died soon after he arrived in America. He was ill on board ship and never fully recovered. He had left her a small annuity but there was nothing else from his family.'

'And the earrings?'

'Hector gave them to Sofia. She hid them in Tish's things because she was

236

scared she would get arrested.'

'And your mother kept them?'

'She struggled with her conscience, debating whether or not to mail them back to Auguste but she didn't want him finding out where she was and in the end she decided to give them to me as a birthday present.

'Of course, she had no idea I would come out here and wear them for Auguste's birthday party.'

The restaurant lurched as a passing speedboat disturbed the restaurant's moorings.

'So there you have it.' May gave a shaky smile.

'Was Auguste disappointed to find out you weren't his granddaughter?'

'I think he was. My mother broke it to him gently that his son was not the love of her life.'

'Poor Auguste, he has suffered a lot of sadness.'

'He's quite upbeat about the situation and agrees it's time we left the past where it belongs and thought about the future.'

'And your plans are?'

'I have promised to stay on here, if you agree.'

'If I agree to what?'

'Florence's departure to Milan means there is a vacancy at the autodromo.'

'You want to take over Florence's job?'

'Yes.'

'But it took you five attempts to pass your driving test.'

'So what? I can drive now. I'm half Italian, and didn't you once offer me a job driving over skid pans or some such when I told you I passed my test in the snow?'

'Yes, but things are different now.'

'Auguste is happy for me to stay on.'

May paused. 'And of course there's us.'

'Us?'

'That relationship talk we had?'

'I think we agreed it wouldn't work.' May relaxed. The worst was over. Vin was no longer glaring at her. 'You know, a part of me always felt out of place with the girls at school. I know now it was because I am half Italian although I didn't realise it at the time. I thought it was because my family was unconventional and I came from a bohemian background, so,' May ploughed on as Vin tried to interrupt, 'I've had a re-think and I feel it would be a good idea if we developed our relationship — that's if you have no objection to being associated with a woman whose mother was once suspected of being a jewel thief and sang for her supper.'

Vin gaped.

'The earrings could be our wedding present from Auguste.'

'You're talking marriage?'

'We would be a powerful team. I can't wait to get stuck in at the autodromo. I've loads of ideas on how to modernise the image.'

'This is not how things are done.' Vin finally managed to get a word in.

'We agreed it's time to move on from the past and I can't hang around waiting for you to make up your mind. I told you I come from a bohemian background

239

and I'm not much of a traditionalist.'

'Have you cooked this up with Auguste?' Vin's eyes narrowed with suspicion.

'I'm sure our marriage would meet with his approval.' May held her breath.

'No.' He shook his head. 'I cannot accept your proposal.'

May's heart sank.

'I hadn't expected you to be so conventional.'

A disturbance from the quayside drew their attention to the water's edge.

'What's your mother doing here?' Vin demanded.

'She's amazing, isn't she? How she can still get into that pink mini dress I do not know.'

'Isn't that Sofia and the Contessa Rosamunde with her?'

'I think it is.'

'Your mother's holding up a bottle of champagne. Have you gone public on this outrageous proposal?'

'Tish was rather hoping you'd say yes. You've made a hit there although she had a few choice words to say about your

240

father, but I'm sure she didn't mean them. She was just getting things out of her system.'

'Perhaps I should ask your mother to marry me,' Vin suggested.

'You wouldn't!' May was appalled at the thought.

'Why not? You've turned tradition on its head.'

'I'll tell Auguste,' May threatened.

'What will he do?'

'Rethink his decision to put you in charge of the autodromo.'

'So you do know of his plans?'

May squirmed.

'He might have hinted but it's isn't official yet.'

'And to clinch the deal you came up with the idea of marriage?'

Tish and Sofia were now precariously balanced on the walkway leading from the quayside to the restaurant.

'Hurry up, darling,' Sofia gestured at May, 'this contraption is not safe.'

'I came up with the idea,' May admitted after a short pause, 'because you stuck by me through thick and thin when everyone else was convinced my mother was guilty of the robberies.'

May's voice gave out on her as Vin leaned back and crossed his arms.

'I did stick by you, didn't I?'

'There's no need to look so self-satisfied.' May knew she sounded crabby but she couldn't contain her disappointment.

'Who is going to break the news to your mother?'

'You can do it.'

Vin looked thoughtful for a moment.

'I think it would make my life a lot easier if you tell her.'

May swallowed the lump in her throat.

'Do it yourself,' was her ungracious reply.

'You could be right, you know. A woman at the helm would create a modern image for the autodromo and who better than the founder's granddaughter?'

'I told you, Auguste is not my grandfather.'

'I expect local gossip will come to its

own conclusion.'

'Well you know the truth but it makes no difference between us, does it? You've turned down my proposal.'

'Can my wedding present to you be one last gig?' Tish's voice rang out from the gangplank.

May turned round to face the trio advancing towards them.

'Tell your mother we accept her offer.'

'What offer?'

'One last gig.'

'But it's a wedding present and you turned down my proposal.'

'Only because I would rather like to do the asking.'

'You mean you're going to be old-fashioned about things?'

'Indulge me,' Vin coaxed. 'Do you think you could live with an old-fashioned man?'

'Why don't you try asking me?' The buzzing noise in May's ears was making concentration difficult.

'Will you marry me?' Vin's eyes bored into May's.

The boat gave another lurch, causing

his proposal to be almost be drowned out
by loud laughter from the neighbouring
tables.

'I think I rather like going traditional,'
May admitted with a shamefaced smile.
'My answer is yes.'

WINGS OF A NIGHTINGALE

Alan C. Williams

It's 1941 when strong-willed Aussie nurse, Pauline Newton, arrives at Killymoor Hall, a British military hospital which has many secrets. Most crucially, it's a base for a team of Nazi saboteurs. Falling in love with the mysterious Sergeant Ray Tennyson, Pauline finds herself involved in murders, skulduggery and intrigue as they both race desperately to discover the German leaders' identity. Throughout it all, Ray and Pauline must resolve their own differences if they hope to stop the Nazis altering the War's outcome forever.

MURDER IN THE HAUNTED CASTLE

Ken Preston

Divorced Kim has come to terms with the fact that her only daughter is growing up. A last memorable holiday together before Maddie immerses herself in GCSE revision seems just the thing. But as if meeting the delectable James (no, not Bond — but close!) isn't exciting enough to throw a spanner in the works, just wait until they all get to the haunted castle. Dream holiday? More like a nightmare! But how will it end . . . ?

ISLAND OF MISTS

Evelyn Orange

Arasay — remote Scottish island, wildlife haven, and home to Jenna's ancestors. When she arrives to help out her great aunt in the bookshop, she's running from her past and hiding from the world. But she's not expecting to meet an attractive wildlife photographer who is also using the island to escape from previous traumas. As Jenna embraces island life and becomes closer to Jake and his family, there are secrets in the mist that could threaten their future happiness . . .

ONE MAN'S LOSS

Valerie Holmes

Sir Christian Leigh-Bolton had never intended to gamble that night the vultures circled around Sir Howard. Losing heavily and in desperation, Sir Howard foolishly wagers away his inheritance, Kingsley Hall — and Christian steps in and wins the prize. Sir Howard's actions leave his sister, Eleanor, virtually homeless. Christian's honour is further tested when he makes a promise to Sir Howard, a dying man, not knowing if he can fulfil it. Meanwhile, Eleanor has taken matters into her own hands . . .

JESSIE'S LITTLE BOOKSHOP BY THE SEA

Kirsty Ferry

Jessie Tempest has two main interests: reading books and selling books. Her little bookshop in the seaside town of Staithes is Jessie's sanctuary from the outside world. When writer Miles Fareham and his inquisitive eight-year-old, Elijah, arrive to stay in the holiday apartment above the shop, it's testing — Jessie has always felt clueless around kids. But soon she realises that first impressions aren't always the right ones — and, of course, you can never judge a book by its cover!